# Lost Tomorrow

## A FEAR & SUNSHINE STORY

Written & Illustrated by
Donovan Scherer

# Dedication

This is for those who sell the popcorn.

# Special Thanks

Jeanne Scherer, Alyssa Archer, Leslie Watts,
Jason Whited, and Walter Ruyeras

# Table of Contents

# A Clockwork Hare

Sunshine ran as fast as she could along the grassy edge of the muddy trail. Surrounded by the rotting husks of ancient trees that stood like long-forgotten towers, she chased the blue rabbit as he spun through the air. She had tossed Bunny too far, too high, and now had to push her legs as hard as she could to reach him before he plummeted into the muck. As easygoing as Pops and Momsy were, Sunshine didn't want to spoil their first picnic in Ballihag Bog by ruining her favorite stuffed animal.

As Bunny descended toward the muddy earth, Sunshine knew it was now or never, so she sprinted to reach him. Feeling the firm surface of an exposed root underfoot, she used it as a springboard and leaped to her stuffed friend. As his button eyes met hers, time seemed to slow down, and she reached out with both hands, grabbing him by the paws.

Sunshine gripped Bunny as she felt herself falling. Her foot hit the muddy ground and slipped. Sunshine fell back. Though she had saved Bunny from his fall, she had doomed herself to a muddy misfortune.

Sunshine landed hard on her back, and it wasn't the slurpy splash she had expected. She peeked up to see Pops holding her in place. Sunshine grinned.

Pops smiled. "You know, Sunshine, if you muddy yourself up, you might be mistaken for a bog monster."

Sunshine straightened herself up and pulled Bunny to her chest. "There are monsters in the swamp?" Her gaze darted back and forth from Pops to Momsy.

Momsy shook her head. "Salvo, you know there are no monsters in the swamp. You're going to get her hopes up."

"Super up!" Sunshine said with a grin stretching from ear to ear. "I would love to meet a monster!"

Momsy laughed and tousled Sunshine's hair. "There are no monsters around here aside from the imaginary ones. It's part of what makes Wandering Willows so great."

Sunshine's shoulders drooped. She could not see what was so great about not having monsters to play with. Though she knew monsters weren't real, she had always dreamed of them. Never too menacing or wanting to eat her alive, the monsters in her dreams were always friendly. Her home with Pops and Momsy in Wandering Willows, where they lived in a house built into the side of a tree, didn't have monsters. It did have plenty of squirrels and the occasional family of deer passing by once in a while.

Momsy looked around, and Sunshine saw her smile. Following her gaze, there was a tall pine tree. The lower branches of the tree, just out of her reach, each had something hanging off of them. As the wind blew, Sunshine realized they were ribbons.

Momsy opened her homemade picnic basket and pulled something out. "Even though there are no monsters, there are plenty of other adventures you can have." She smiled as she handed the rolled up piece of paper to Sunshine.

Sunshine looked in wonder at the pale-blue ribbon that held the paper in place. It was the same kind as those hanging above them from the tree. She peered at it, sure that the matching ribbon was no coincidence.

"Go ahead," Momsy said. "It's a gift."

Handing Bunny to Pops, Sunshine took one of the loose ends of the ribbon in hand. She pulled and unrolled the document, slowly revealing just what she had hoped for.

Sunshine felt bubbles of delight fluttering in her belly as she saw a hand-drawn legend belonging to a map in the bottom corner of the unrolled parchment. Right below that were the words, "Love, Auntie Constance."

She let out a brief squeal as she opened the map all the way. Sitting at the top of the page was "Ballihag Bog," and just below it in smaller lettering, "Home of secrets, bog monsters, and unknown treasure." Littering the page were icons of trees and various points of interest, a squiggly line showing the southern path they had already walked along from their house, and then more squiggles of trails connecting everywhere to everything.

Sunshine beamed as she looked from Momsy to Pops then back again. Her shoulders rose up, nearly to her ears, and she was ready to find the secrets that Wandering Willows hid away in its northern marsh.

"Well, Flora?" Pops said to Momsy like he was asking for permission.

"I suppose so."

Sunshine watched in silence as Momsy reached down and stretched out a single finger. The finger slowly moved toward the map in Sunshine's hands until, finally, it landed on three little words: "You are here."

Sunshine pulled Bunny by the paw as she skipped into the marshland, leaving Pops and Momsy to set up a site for their lunchtime picnic. On both sides of the path were small pools of shallow swamp water that let out occasional bubbles and gurgles from whatever strange life existed beneath the surface. The air smelled like baked beans, one of Sunshine's favorite foods, and she breathed it in deeply, hoping to catch the scent of a new clue for her adventure.

She sighed and made a puzzled face at the world around her. In the middle of the path ahead sat one large tree with its roots exposed and jutting into the water beyond its small plot of land. Its long hanging leaves dipped all the way to the ground. She walked to the trunk of the tree and squatted down beside it. Setting Bunny in front of her, she unraveled the map and laid it out between them.

"Hmm," Sunshine said. "I can't catch a sniff of it, but we should be at this picture here, I think." She pointed at a field of flowers. "You don't think we're lost already, do you?"

Bunny didn't reply, but Sunshine took his silence as his usual stoic wisdom and stood back up. "You're right," she said. "We're never lost as long as we can un-lose where we are. So, we just have to figure out where that is."

Sunshine picked up Bunny and the map, taking one more look at it. Then, finding the last landmark they had passed (a group of three trees that had grown into each other thirty feet above the ground), she nodded.

"We'll head back there and straighten ourselves out," she told Bunny. "No sense in going deeper into the swamp and getting more lost."

Sunshine took a moment to get her bearings. In the distance, she could see where the tree line opened up. Beyond the section of forest she stood in, long-dead trees—the remnants of either age or a forest fire—stood tall and scattered like tombstones in a poorly managed graveyard. Sunshine stood up tall on her toes. She spun around and took the first step back the way they came. But before her foot landed, she froze.

A silver streak had flashed in her vision. Her gaze darted back and forth, trying to catch another glimpse. A branch snapped, and she twisted toward the sound. Nothing. Then, the silvery flash appeared from nowhere and shot back the other way. She spun, again too slowly.

"Bunny," she whispered, squeezing him tight. "We're not alone."

Sunshine could feel the presence of something, maybe many somethings, watching her. She tried to see, tried to listen, but then the thing came into view and vanished just as quickly.

"Is it the bog monster?" Sunshine asked Bunny through trembling lips.

As she tried to imagine what the swamp-dwelling menace looked like, something didn't add up. Why would a bog monster be made of something shiny like metal? Sunshine shook her head. Whatever this thing was, it didn't belong in Ballihag Bog. It didn't belong in any part of the Wandering Willows.

Sunshine turned to the path leading back to Pops and Momsy. With a quick a look back and forth, she saw nothing. If there was a time to escape, it was now.

Sunshine leaped forward into a sprint. On the other side of the pond, she could see the silver streak running parallel to her. She tried to ignore it, keeping her eyes on the three, grown-together trees. She could hear the branches snapping and metallic joints clamoring as the invader of the marsh moved closer. She pushed herself harder, trying to move even faster than her feet had ever carried her, to get back to the safety of her foster parents.

The bright flash of silver flew in front of her. Then, right in between her and the three towering trees, it stopped. Sunshine slowed, her heart thumping hard.

Although the metal creature didn't entirely resemble Bunny, it was most definitely some kind of rabbit. The black mesh panel it had in place of a nose twitched as it stared at Sunshine. Its eyes glowed white, their brightness pulsing with life. One eye had a thick, dark-gray ring around it that looked like the monocle Pops would sometimes wear when working on projects at home. One of those projects, though it never worked, was something Pops called a robot.

"Are you a robot?" Sunshine asked as she clutched Bunny.

The silver hare continued to stare at her without answer. As Sunshine took one slow footstep after another, she heard a ticking sound. With each step, though the silver hare seemed expressionless, the tick-tocking grew louder.

She stopped. The noise coming from the hare clicked faster and faster. Whatever gears made up its insides were working at full capacity. Sunshine's feet dug into the ground. If the hare was about to burst into overdrive, she was ready to launch right after it. The sound reached its peak and then stopped. Sunshine and the robot stared at each other.

Within a blink, the silver hare stood up on its hind legs. Sunshine gasped as she saw that it was nearly as tall as she was. It wore clothes: a white buttoned shirt (which appeared to be tucked into a metal seam at its waist), a pair of green-and-yellow checkered suspenders, and a matching plastic bow tie.

Sunshine stepped forward and stretched out her arms, holding Bunny toward the machine.

"This is Bunny," Sunshine said, her voice weak.

And then the robot was gone, leaving only a trail of silver behind.

"Wait!" Sunshine yelled, chasing after the robot. "I'll name you Barney! Barney the Silver Blur of Ballihag!"

Once again, she spotted the silver flashes of light disappearing and reappearing in the distance. Instead of any sense of dread, Sunshine's belly was filled with delight. She had just found someone new to join her and Bunny's adventures.

Barney led Sunshine in circles through the swamp, over fallen trees, through thick and greasy muck, past ragged bushes, and in and out of vines that stretched from all around then up to the canopy above. Sunshine, as quick as she was with Bunny in tow, kept falling short whenever it looked like she was about to get to the clockwork hare. But despite the hopelessness of her pursuit, the excitement inside her grew.

Sunshine saw the silver streak glide through thorny vines. When she reached them, the vines themselves seemed to come alive. They lashed toward her, and she laughed as she jumped out of their grasp. When Barney reappeared, leaping over a clump of bushes, she imagined it as a giant, yellow-freckled bullfrog croaking at its unwelcome visitor. She ran alongside one of the dark ponds, watching the silver hare skip across the surface with amazing speed. She pictured the massive heads of mustachioed carp breaking the surface of the water as they tried to grab him like a bug.

Sunshine twirled around, watching the new world come to life around her. Magical, monstrous creatures, all coming from her imagination, filled the swamp. But then she heard something else.

Sunshine turned toward the sound but found nothing. In the distance, she saw something oddly familiar. A stack of rocks towered as high as the treetops, but she hadn't seen anything like them in Ballihag Bog.

She saw where some of the stones had fallen out of place, leaving what looked like a pair of vacant eye sockets in a giant stone owl. As it stared back at Sunshine, she remembered where she had seen something similar.

Sunshine ran to the side of the path and crouched alongside a bush. She unrolled the map and pulled Bunny up so they both could see. There, in the upper corner, was the stone owl. To the lower left of the owl, she saw another strange animal figure.

Sunshine stood and looked to the left of the owl. She located the other stack of stones, this one in a bit better condition than the owl. It looked like a fish leaping straight up out of the water. It was actually farther away than the owl was, almost twice as far. Sunshine tried to determine just how the distance related to inches on the map. Then, she heard the noise again.

Unlike the mechanical whirring sound of Barney, this sounded like something that was truly alive. Unfortunately, it sounded hungry. Chasing the robot would have to wait. Though she still couldn't tell what the source of the hungry groans was, Sunshine grabbed Bunny and the map and ran.

She knew that if she headed toward the fish, she would be headed in the direction of Pops and Momsy, but every time she ran, she heard the growling sound somewhere ahead of her. Barney continued to appear in and out of Sunshine's line of sight, if only as a beam of light. She tried to watch the robot running circles around her, and tried to find the unseen creature hunting her, but spinning around while trying to find them both only made her dizzy.

Watching the silver streak, she saw that it kept moving from right to left and realized it made a big, counterclockwise circle around her. Looking back and beyond a small cluster of trees, Sunshine saw the far side of Barney's path and found another statue—a bear made of flat stacked stones. With her path blocked in all directions by the mysterious growling and the silver trail of light closing in tighter and tighter around her, there was nowhere Sunshine could go outside of the three statues.

She ran toward a cluster of trees in the center of the statues. If she couldn't escape, she could at least try to hide. As she ran, it felt like the statues had started moving, closing in on her. Sunshine squeezed Bunny, and then, reaching the trees, she jumped.

Sunshine slid through the mud into a small opening in one of the tree trunks. Aside from her own heartbeat, she couldn't hear anything, not the whirring sound of the silver hare and not the hungry growl of the animal tracking her. Despite the welcome calm, she knew she wasn't safe. She knew there was nothing she could do but hide and wait until Pops and Momsy came looking for her. She only hoped they wouldn't be too late.

With Bunny in her lap, Sunshine took out the map and looked it over. She quickly found the new statue, the bear, and even found the trees that she now hid in. Then, she felt as though the breath was sucked out of her chest as she saw the words beneath the drawing of trees.

"Home of the Ballihag Bog Monster."

Sunshine looked around the inside of the tree. She reached out to touch the claw marks on the walls. Then, running her fingers along some strange, ancient-looking carvings, each no bigger than her hand, she smiled.

"Well," she said to Bunny, "at least we know the bog monster isn't very big. There's hardly room for the two of us in here."

Sunshine leaned back and pressed her feet up on the wall in front of her.

"I suppose all we can do is wait."

Sunshine stared at the claw marks around her, wondering what the bog monster looked like. After blinking a few times, her eyes soon closed. Waiting for something to happen was always a good time to nap.

Then, everything became very, very warm.

# Lost Tomorrow

# The Empty Road

Sunshine's eyes opened with a jolt. She didn't understand what was happening, but her whole body felt like it was wrapped up tight in a hundred blankets and she was sitting in front of a fireplace. It wasn't entirely uncomfortable, but it didn't make any sense. Then, like someone wrapped up in those hundred blankets, she struggled as she tried to move her arms.

Panicking, Sunshine looked down. Bunny was gone. Her body was gone. She could see only mud. It was all around her, all the way up to her shoulders.

Sunshine was sinking.

"Bog monster trap!" Sunshine yelled.

As she struggled, she sank faster and faster. She could wiggle less and less as the muddy hole consumed her. She could feel the mud rising, herself sinking, as the warm muck reached her neck.

Beneath the mud, Sunshine could still feel Bunny in her hands. She tried to pull him closer but could barely even move her fingers. As the mud touched the bottom of her chin, she turned her head back and forth, desperately trying to find anything that would help. But even if there was something to grab onto, she couldn't pull her hands up from the mud. She was helpless. Finally, hoping that Pops and Momsy may be near, Sunshine screamed for help.

Out of nowhere, Barney stood at the entrance to the tree trunk of doom. Sunshine blinked through tears.

"Please," she begged.

The robot's white eyes now glowed green as he stared at her, not responding. He moved closer, as if to sniff Sunshine.

*Beep. Beep. Blurp. Beep.*

Sunshine sniffed. "I don't talk robot."

Barney beeped again then stepped back. Lowering to all four feet, he put his nose down to the ground. Sunshine watched as he pressed his nose deeper and deeper.

The robot's head completely submerged, just like most of Sunshine. She didn't understand why the thing wouldn't just pull her up. And then, the robot's arms started spinning. He was digging.

Sunshine closed one eye, trying to block the flinging mud as it spattered the inside of the tree trunk. Soon, the robot was completely underground. She wasn't sure what was happening. Why would Barney join her in this fate rather than help her out of it?

She stayed still, hoping that would help slow her sinking. She tried to feel for something happening underground. Maybe the robot went to push her up from the bottom instead of trying to pull her up. Barney did have very small paws, after all.

Sunshine waited.

And waited.

She tipped her chin up as the mud reached her mouth. With still no sign of the robot trying to help, Sunshine tightened her lips as mud covered them. She squeezed Bunny with all the strength she could muster beneath the mud. One last breath, deep through her nose. Sunshine closed her eyes.

Then, nothing.

And in that nothing, she wiggled her toes. She wiggled her foot.

Then, she wiggled both feet. She wiggled them faster. Sunshine could feel the mud finally cover the top of her head, but the nothing she felt at her feet was all that mattered. The faster she wiggled them, the more she was able to move. Soon, her leg was free all the way up to her knee. She pushed through the mud, stretching out every limb with all her strength.

When sitting inside the tree trunk, she had been curled up tight. She had stayed that way while she sank, but now, with her arms and legs spread out as far as they could go, Sunshine felt the freedom of air beneath her. The muddy floor, or ceiling to whatever waited beneath, opened, and it seemed to be the only way she could go.

Still holding her breath, her legs kicked back and forth, pulling her down faster. Her feet still felt nothing, but falling into whatever depths awaited was a more welcome option than suffocating in a muddy tomb.

With most of her body hanging, she sank even faster. Soon, she fell free. Sunshine gasped as she heard the sucking, slurping sound of the mud pulling back together above her. Despite the relief of being able to breath, she was still falling.

Sunshine's back hit something, and she bounced. Plummeting once again, she spun around midair to face down into a pit. In the darkness, a few lights glowed and blinked and pulsed, just like Barney's eyes. Though the light was dim, she could see what looked like thick rope stretching from wall to wall.

Tucking Bunny beneath one arm, Sunshine reached out. She caught it with the crook of her elbow, wincing from the sudden shock that the rope wasn't a rope at all. It was bouncy but hard, with a metal wrapping around it. Sunshine had played with small wires before, having gathered a fine collection of scraps from some of Pops' work, but those wires were tiny, not the heavy-duty cable she found here. Hanging in the air, she looked down. She could see lots of the cables and multicolored lights. Unfortunately, she couldn't see the bottom.

Kicking her legs up around the cable she hung from, Sunshine got a better grip. Above her, she saw the muddy ceiling. She must have fallen fifteen feet, and the only thing between her and the mud was the first cable she'd hit on the way down. That cable and the one she clung to now came straight out from the wall, a wall with no ladders, stairs, or any way to get back up to Ballihag Bog.

Sunshine looked down. Then she looked at Bunny. She held her breath for a moment, knowing there was only one thing to do.

"You know when we climb too high in a tree and we have to come down but I can't carry you because I need my hands?"

Bunny stared at her.

"Well, this is kind of like that."

Bunny didn't answer.

"Only this time, I don't really know where the ground is, so I need you to figure that out. Okay?"

Still no reply, but Sunshine knew Bunny had accepted his duty.

"Here we go."

Sunshine let go of Bunny and watched him fall into the darkness. As he fell from sight, she tried to listen for a thud. There were a couple of bumps as he hit what Sunshine assumed were more cables, but not the thud she hoped to hear. She waited.

And waited.

Nothing.

The only way left to go was down. Sunshine, hanging from the cable, turned her head to try and see what was below her. After listening for Bunny's descent into the darkness, Sunshine knew that if she did let go, she'd have at least some chance of finding another cable to cling onto before splattering on the ground, however far down that may be. She shimmied to the middle of the cable so that her weight would make it droop as low as possible. Then, she wrapped her legs around it as tightly as she could.

Sunshine let go with her hands, letting herself fall back to see the world upside down while she kept hold of the cable with her legs. Something inside her mind, probably the thought of what Pops and Momsy would say about this whole idea, nagged at her. She couldn't see the next cable, had no idea where to aim her fall, and wasn't even sure if she'd be able to catch a handhold on her way down.

She pulled herself back up. This was a bad idea.

"Bunny!" Sunshine yelled. "I'm going to try and find a way back up! I'll bring help and come right back to get you!"

Expecting silence, Sunshine gasped when she heard something shuffle then beep. Just below her, she saw the green, glowing eyes of the silver hare. The eyes blinked at her then disappeared. Sunshine heard a thud then a rustling, and there the eyes were again, this time lower into the pit, but not too far down for her to safely drop. Sunshine watched as the robot kept descending and listened to its motor whir. Now she knew just where to go.

Slowly, Sunshine made her way deeper, falling from one cable to the next as she followed Barney, clinging tightly to each as she had no idea how far down the pit went. Occasional lights outlined the pit, blinking or pulsing with electricity. The buzzing and beeps grew more and more common as she descended. They reminded her of Barney, but these sounds were fainter, more like a wheezing chatter than whirring.

As more lights came into view, so did more of the pit. Sunshine could see the walls of it widening. Oddly, she still had no idea where she would find the bottom.

Sunshine saw Barney on the next cable. He seemed to be waiting for her to catch up. Now the different-colored lights filled the pit, and Sunshine looked past the robot. She realized why Barney had stopped. They had reached the final cable.

Sunshine released her grip and fell down to join him. Barney sat on the top and wobbled as Sunshine steadied herself. She tried to see the bottom, hoping to find Bunny, but something about the ground didn't seem right.

The light around the pit reflected back up in strange waves. As neon blue and yellow and red light swirled around the ground far below her, Sunshine couldn't figure out what she was looking at. The only thing she did know was that Bunny was somewhere down there waiting for her.

"What do we do now?" she asked, looking up at the silver hare.

The robot's nose twitched as he stared at her. The light reflecting in swirls on the ground did the same on Barney's metal hide. Then, he leaned over the side of the cable. Waiting or looking for something, the hare stayed still.

Sunshine's head whipped back as he leaped into the neon abyss. He fell into the light and quickly disappeared from sight. Sunshine pulled herself up onto the cable and braced herself. She looked down toward the bottom of the pit. She saw where Barney had aimed, but he was gone now. His lights appeared across the pit's bottom then disappeared into more emptiness before flashing one final time.

As other lights danced from here to there, patterns slowly revealed themselves. Sunshine could see that the ground was metal, smooth, and sloped just enough that she might be able to slide down without breaking her neck. It was time to fall.

Sunshine pushed herself up to a tall, seated position with both legs hanging over one side of the cable. Holding her breath as she tried to maintain her balance, she looked down. It was very far, and whenever the light moved, it looked like there was nothing below her at all.

Sunshine held her breath and let go.

She winced as she hit the hard metal surface. Blue light flashed in her eyes, then red, then yellow. She had reached the bottom, but she was still falling … or sliding.

As she slid, Sunshine tried to grab onto anything to stop herself. Nothing was within reach. As the slide continued, the angle seemed to get steeper and steeper, and she moved faster and faster.

Abruptly, the swirling lights vanished. Sunshine descended into total darkness. She could feel nothing but the heat of the friction on her back and arms as she slid. As she zipped from one side of the slanted surface to the other, a grin stretched across Sunshine's face. She had never been on any sort of ride that was more fun than this.

Sunshine laughed as she rocketed down the slide. When she hit a bump, she managed to spin herself just a bit then twist onto her stomach so she could go headfirst. It felt like flying.

She imagined soaring high above the trees of Wandering Willows but finally felt herself slowing down. Bumps on the slide became more and more frequent until it leveled off to the flat ground. Sunshine boosted herself up to her feet and spun in circles with her arms wide open thanks to the momentum that left her feeling like she had wings. She was a bit disappointed that the ride had come to an end.

Though it was hard to see with the darkness broken only by an occasional flicker of electric lights, Sunshine discovered that she'd landed in a completely new world. She could make out the outlines of buildings in the distance. They were huge, bigger than even the biggest trees on top of the highest hills in Wandering Willows. However, something about them, maybe the emptiness all around or the stale taste in the air, made Sunshine feel like she was the only thing alive in this cavernous underground world.

Sunshine looked back at the structure that had brought her here. The slide went all the way up into the impenetrable blackness. As smooth as it had felt on the way down, the metal looked cobbled together from a bajillion pieces of scrap. Looking right and left, she saw that it wasn't a slide at all. It was a wall.

The metal wall seemed to go on endlessly, from side to side and all the way up. She could make out hulking masses of metal at the base of the wall. It was hard to tell with the things being tipped on their side, but they were giant ships rested beside parts of the wall, their hulls ripped apart. Sunshine looked at the wreckage, then the metal wall, and realized that whoever did this must have liked building walls much more than playing on boats.

Sunshine turned from the wall to see what she could see. She smiled when the first thing she spotted was her best friend. Skipping through the dimness, Sunshine scooped up Bunny and spun him around.

"Pretty weird place, huh?" Sunshine asked the stuffed rabbit. "No worries. Any place as weird as this must be a dream. We'll just explore until we wake up."

Reunited with her friend, Sunshine turned toward the abandoned city that was obviously a result of today's overworked imagination. She had never seen so much concrete and metal before. The buildings here were monstrosities towering above her, all very square and boring. A place like this seemed unnatural. Her home with Pops and Momsy was simple, wooden, and built into a tree like any good home ought to be.

Rubble filled the streets. She heard no sounds of people or animals or nature. Aside from the pulsing of a few scattered lights, she couldn't detect any type of motion, not even wind. She saw a huge old poster dangling lifelessly from a giant rectangular stand. It was even bigger than the mural Momsy had painted on the ceiling of their living room. Still visible from the tattered remains, half the face of a young, smiling boy looked back at Sunshine. Above him in print, it read, "Welcome to the World of Tomorrow!"

Whatever world this city belonged to reminded Sunshine of the tree stump that sat down the road from her home. Though you could tell what it once was, the stump was far from the tree it used to be. At least that stump had bugs living in it.

Sunshine's footsteps echoed as she walked down the empty road that led into the city. Broken windows seemed to outnumber the ones that were still intact. Signs were posted everywhere, along the streets and on the buildings, but all were faded to the point of being unreadable. Whatever had happened here, happened a long, long time ago.

Then, Sunshine heard something familiar. She turned toward the buzzing sound and saw the silver hare. He stared at her, and though its glowing eyes, once again white, pulsed, he seemed unaware of her presence.

"Hey," Sunshine yelled. "How do we get back home?"

Barney didn't respond. Not even a beep.

"Oh, come on. This place is super spooky. Pops and Momsy are probably real worried about me."

Again, Barney ignored her. Then, turning his head, the silver streak shot off into distance and disappeared from sight.

"Well," Sunshine said to herself.

Sunshine looked up and down the street, trying to find some clue as to the direction to go. With the signs all faded or covered in who-knew-how-many years of dust, there wasn't much to work with. She walked down the middle of the road, making her way down the block. The lights, rare as they were, were about as bright as moonlight. It was enough to guide her along the trip but left plenty of shadows to worry her.

Then, a few blocks down the road, Sunshine saw a slightly brighter orange spot of light. Sunshine put Bunny on top of her head and pulled his legs down around her ears. This probably wasn't a way back home, but the dead city didn't seem to have much else to offer.

# Signs of Life

Sunshine hugged Bunny as she walked down the road toward the only sign of life. The orange light, still a couple of blocks down the road, cast shadows across the front of the buildings that lined the street. The shadows moved in circles, dancing around her as she walked into the unknown.

Some of the walls of buildings had posters hanging from them. Even though time had faded the artwork, Sunshine could tell that some had been printed and some were handmade.

"The end is nigh," Sunshine read aloud, unsure what "nigh" meant. Then, seeing another poster with an illustration of strange, wide-mouthed creatures and the words "Coming Soon" above it, Sunshine laughed.

"They look like little bog monsters."

Her walk took her past more and more piles of rubble, tattered papers in the street, and broken windows. Everything looked like a storm had once blown through the city and then nothing had ever happened again.

Sunshine had never seen so many of the things lying around in the street. Before the haunting deadness that filled it now, this place must have been incredible. Strange devices and plastic toys littered the ground, long forgotten by their owners. Vehicles with long sleek bodies, very unlike (but still sort of similar to) the clunky truck she had once found abandoned in the forest near her house were all over the road. Like that truck, all of their rubber tires were deflated and looked like empty sacks. Their windows were so covered in grime and dust that Sunshine couldn't see inside, and the feeling in her stomach made her not even want to.

The buildings were amazing things to see. Sunshine imagined some of the towers would take at least a day just to climb up. In the glow of some of the few lights high overhead, she could see that the tops of some of the tallest buildings were built directly into the metal shell that wrapped all around the city.

She had always loved tinkering with odds and ends, especially with Pops, to make new things. She knew that the little pieces of scrap they found could be added to this or that to create something new. With the right tools, they could make anything. However, the scope of ingenuity she saw around her now, despite the fact that this place was lost long ago, made her smile. Then, the ground around Sunshine's feet glowed.

"What in the world of tomorrow is going on now?"

Since she'd not been paying attention while walking, she only now realized she had made it to the source of the orange light she'd been traveling toward.

Sitting on top of a building, smaller than all the rest around it, something about the glowing "BB" sign felt warm and inviting. Sunshine smiled, seeing smaller unlit signs all around the building featuring a grinning cartoon horse eating some kind of sandwich. She wasn't sure why that would be a thing, but she couldn't help but giggle. And though she assumed it was still early, something about the faded pictures of the horse made her feel very ready for lunch.

"Bunny," Sunshine said, "I think we found a place to get a snack!"

Sunshine ran to the building. All around it were large glass windows, all of them too dirty to see inside. She ran toward a door and, in her hurry, crashed into it, laughing at herself. As she pulled the handle, her chuckle stopped. The doors were locked.

Sunshine wiped at the glass door to clean away enough grime to peek through. She looked inside, seeing a few lights but no sign of movement. On the wall behind a long counter was another illuminated sign with the horse eating a sandwich.

After giving one last hopeless tug at the door handle, Sunshine backed away, her head hanging.

"I would have liked to meet that horse," she said to Bunny.

Sunshine walked away from the door, keeping an eye on the section of glass she had cleaned off, still hoping for a chance that there was something inside that she could have as a snack. Finally turning away, she saw the steel fence that came from one side of the building and wrapped around its yard.

Sunshine skipped up to the fence. Inside she saw three of the same horses from the sign, though these were small and had fat springs holding them up from the ground. They all had saddles as well, and were the perfect size for Sunshine to ride. Behind the horses was a set of swings, a weird cage that would probably be loads of fun to climb in and out of, and a long slide that spiraled and hooked left and right on its way down, similar to the giant one that brought her to this world.

As she made her way along the fence, she looked for some way to get inside. Beside the things to play on, there were more doors to the building that might be unlocked. However, and despite the small park appearing to be built for children, all along the top of the fence was coiled wire with long sharp barbs sticking out of it. She tried to see to the other end of the fence, hoping to find a gate, but then the hair stood up on the back of her neck. Sunshine froze in place.

Sunshine stayed still, staring at the motionless figure. Boney hands still gripped the fence after who-knows-how-many years, and held the skeleton in place as its empty eye sockets stared into the void.

"Hello?" Sunshine whispered.

She knew she wouldn't get a response but had to say something. Though she had seen dead animals before, mostly bugs that had accidentally been smashed under her feet, she had never seen a dead person. Squeezing Bunny even tighter, Sunshine walked up to the skeleton. She looked in the direction it was staring then back to its cold, decayed face.

"What happened to you?"

Sunshine stepped away from the fence. Even if she could get into the playground, she would rather not play while the skeleton stood watch. On the narrow road that wrapped around the fence, Sunshine took one last look at the building. It had been the only sign of life in the city, but it was clearly dead, too.

Sunshine turned and walked, not paying any attention to where she went. She didn't know where to go, what to do, or how to get back to Pops and Momsy. She had stumbled into a world unlike anything she had imagined, and there was simply nothing here for her.

Then, she tripped.

"*Bzzzt*. Welcome to Binjo Burger! Are you excited to try our *bzzzt* Chip Mighty Burger Combo Meal with Double *bzzzt* and Super Salsa?"

The voice came from above her. Sunshine looked up into yet another frozen face of the grinning horse.

"Hello?" Sunshine asked, picking herself up while staring at the horse. On each side of the horse's wide grin, two large panels stood, both with the "BB" logo mounted on top. Though they had a layer of grime covering them, same as all the windows she had seen, she could make out various pictures of food.

"*Bzzzt* What can I get you today?"

Sunshine looked at the pictures, but despite the urge to snack, knew there were other questions she needed to ask.

"Where am I?"

"You're at *bzzzt* Binjo Burger, of course. Our meals are *bzzzt* deals; you'd call them real steals! Would you like to try one of *bzzzt* combo meals today?"

Sunshine shrugged. "Sure. How do I get back home?"

"Home is where the hungry is! What kind *bzzzt* you *bzzzt*?"

She looked through the smears on the glass. "A number three, I guess. What happened here?"

After a moment of silence. "Oh, I'm sorry. *Bzzzt* all out of that one. Would you like to try again?"

"Number four." Sunshine walked up to the board and looked around the side of it. "Are you inside the building? Are you a person?"

"*Bzzzt* person? Of course! Oh, I'm sorry. We're all out of that *bzzzt*. Would you like to try again?"

Sunshine looked back at the front of the menu. "Number seven. If you're a person, where are you?"

"A person? Of course! Welcome to Binjo Burger! Oh, I'm sorry. We're all *bzzzt* of that one. Would you like to try again?"

Sunshine rolled her eyes. "What do you have?"

The moment of silence returned.

"It appears that we're completely out of stock. Congratulations! Welcome to Binjo Burger! How may I help you?"

Sunshine let out an exaggerated exhale. "I'm pretty sure you're not really a person."

"A person? Of course! Oh, I'm sorry. We're all … Binjo Burger … out of … home of the … are you excited to … *WARNING. WARNING. Please return bzzzt your homes* … Are you excited to … "

Sunshine stared at the smiling horse face and frowned as she realized there would be no snacks today. The chatter continued incoherently.

"Hey!" Sunshine interrupted the talking box. "If you don't have any food, at least answer a question for me!"

"Of course," the horse said, breaking away from its rambling. "How may I help you today?"

Sunshine paused, trying to think of a question that wouldn't trigger nonsense. She looked at Bunny then to the world around her.

"Where is everyone?"

The machine hesitated, searching its programming for an appropriate response. Then, without warning, an alarm blared out from the speaker.

*"WARNING. WARNING. Please return to your homes. This is not a drill. Mandatory evacuation deadline has passed. Please return to your homes. You will be notified once the situation returns to normal. WARNING. WARN-ING. This is not a drill."*

Sunshine hugged Bunny, turning his button eyes away from the grinning horse.

"Is everyone gone?"

The horse didn't answer.

"Hello?"

"Welcome to *bzzzt* Burger! Are you *bzzzt* to *bzzzt* our *bzzzt bzzzt bzzzt* … "

Sunshine stomped her foot. "You! You are not very helpful!"

"Oh, I'm *bzzzt*! It is *bzzzt* duty to give you a happy *bzzzt*. Customer satisfaction is our number one *bzzzt*! Please, enjoy two *bzzzt* tickets for *bzzzt* local cinema, located only three *bzzzt* away. Would you *bzzzt* to try one of our *bzzzt* today?"

Below the speaker, two pieces of paper slid out of a slot. Ignoring the horse, Sunshine pulled the tickets and looked at them.

"Enjoy a complimentary movie, courtesy of Binjo Burger … "

Sunshine walked away from the board and kept going until the mechanical voice faded away. Climbing on top of a picnic table, Sunshine sat down and put Bunny in her lap. She looked at the tickets. Unsure of what a cinema was, Sunshine was intrigued. On the tickets, a cartoon hot dog and paper cup, both with the same absurd grin as the Binjo Burger horse, made it look like a place to have fun. And hopefully, a talking hot dog would be more helpful than a horse.

"Well," she said, "I suppose we can go see what a movie is."

After looking over the tiny map on the back of the ticket and fig-uring out which road to take, Sunshine set out to find the cinema. Holding the tickets in one hand and Bunny's paw in the other, Sunshine kept a slow pace as she headed down the road. After hearing the warning spouted out by the horse, the city was cast in a whole new light. Something terrible, however long ago, had hap-pened here.

As she walked, Sunshine noticed that her footsteps sounded funny. Each step fell flat, leaving no echo in the still air. As she passed the first block from Binjo Burger, more husks of buildings stood around her. They didn't make her feel unsafe, but she was eager to leave them behind.

"We should probably hurry and wake up," she said to Bunny. "I think this isn't a place for people to be anymore."

Sunshine quickened her pace. Though she had no idea how to end this dream, maybe the cinema would hold some clue.

In the distance, she could see the silhouette of a building. It was set back from a huge open area full of all different kinds of auto-mobiles. The vastness of the empty space was a strange sight after coming across so many buildings pressed up against each other on the way. She could also see a faint white sign standing out from the darkness. Towering above that was a sign that looked like a spire desperately trying to stand out among the nearby buildings.

As Sunshine walked between the vehicles, the lights above her turned on, awakened by her presence. After the fourth light, the rest of them, leading all the way to the building, flickered on. Then, Sunshine stood still and watched in awe as the building itself woke from the desolate world around it.

First, the spire lit up. One by one, bulbs glowed from top to bottom along the sides of the building's sign. Then, the bright letters turned on. "ACADEMY" was spelled out in red from top to bottom on the spire, and cast its light across the glass and metal of the parked automobiles. More lights brightened, outlining the entire building. And finally, the marquee itself slowly shone its brilliant bright white.

Sunshine ran toward the cinema. The multicolored lights reminded her of Momsy's garden in full bloom and were something this city desperately needed. This was the first thing in the city that she felt happy to see.

"The Return of the Muck-Mouths," Sunshine read aloud. It was the only name on the marquee that was not missing letters or covered in grime.

She looked at the tickets in her hand then to Bunny. "This doesn't look so bad."

As Sunshine approached the building, piano music started to play from inside. The melody made it less of a shock when she saw her second skeleton for the day, this one leaning against the counter in a small closed-in room centered between the building's doors. Something about it being hunched over the counter reminded her of Pops working on some afternoon project. Knowing how much her foster dad loved bringing his ideas to life, she could only imagine that whoever this was had died doing something they enjoyed.

Then, thinking of what Momsy would say if she had walked in, Sunshine smiled.

"Working hard or hardly working?"

The skeleton ignored her.

As Sunshine stepped closer, the doors burst open and the music blared out. Sunshine laughed, surprised by the explosion of sound, and then waved at the skeleton inside the ticket booth as she skipped into the cinema.

Unlike the building's exterior, the lights inside the lobby hadn't yet returned to life. Standing in the darkness, she hummed along with the music. Waiting for the lights to come on as they had outside, Sunshine heard something moving toward her.

The sound quickly grew louder as it moved closer. Squinting at the darkness, she was unable to see anything. She stepped back, hitting the door, which had automatically closed behind her. The sound rushed toward her. She squeezed Bunny, shrank against the door, and braced for impact. For some reason—maybe desperation, maybe just confusion—her hand shot forward, holding out the tickets.

# Lost Tomorrow

# Sneak Preview

The high-pitched squeal filled Sunshine's ears as a large squarish silhouette stopped in front of her. Peeking out from behind Bunny, all she could see was a red beam of light that moved up and down to scan her. Though she didn't feel it, she still tried to wipe it away.

"Right on time," said a voice from behind the light. It was higher pitched than the Binjo horse's voice but had a similar mechanical sound like it came through a speaker. "The film is about to start!"

Lights throughout the lobby glowed to life. Lines of bulbs, just like around the outside of the building, outlined a sign with huge white letters that read: "CONCESSIONS." Small robots, no bigger than squirrels, began scurrying behind it, readying themselves to serve their customer. Large glass-walled contraptions with pictures of popcorn across a sign at the top powered on. Inside them, automated arms loaded metal kettles with oil and kernels.

More music started to play as arcade games along the walls fired up to join the frenzy. Sunshine's heart thumped in her chest as everything around her became livelier than anything she had ever seen. It couldn't be more different than the dead world outside.

The robot's digital face appeared on a screen where its head should be and was almost cartoonish with its ridiculous grin in between the two antennae jutting out from the side of its head. Just like Barney, this robot wore a checkered bowtie and matching suspenders. Sunshine had no idea why the theater usher was wearing suspenders, since instead of pants, the bottom half of the machine was one big upside-down dome with a single wheel there to hold it upright.

"Welcome, welcome," the robot said. "I'll be your Usher-Bot while you're a guest at Academy Cinemas. Before we begin, I must ask: Are you ready for the best cinematic experience of your life?"

"I think so," Sunshine said. "But I should really hurry up and get back home."

"Ah, little human. Once you see our wide selection of box office hits, there will be no place you'd rather call home than the movies."

The Usher-Bot rolled closer to Sunshine and leaned down, its digital smile stretching even wider.

"Now tell me, what's your favorite movie?"

Sunshine's averted her gaze from the face of the robot. "Umm. I've never seen a movie."

The Usher-Bot tilted backward and spun its wheel in shock.

"A first-timer? Well, well, well. In that case, welcome to a whole new world. A world where you can sit back, relax, and let the wonders of Tinseltown wash over your delightful little human brain."

A tube shot out of the robot's side, right where an arm ought to be. Using it to point the way, he then led her to the concession stand and pointed up to a small dark screen on the other side, next to the popcorn machine.

"Let's see what we have," the Usher-Bot said as another arm burst out from his side. Small claws grew from the end and then tapped at a panel on his chest.

Sunshine watched the small screen on the wall blink on, and the name "Academy Cinemas" appeared. Sunshine ran up to concession stand to get a closer look.

"In a world," a deep voice boomed. Sunshine watched as images of cities flashed on the screen. They looked to be much like the one she was in now but were full of life and color. People were happy, doing their day-to-day business. But then, chaos. Explosions erupted in the streets, and people ran in panic. The music turned sinister.

"We thought we were safe," the deep voice said. "We thought they were gone."

Sunshine shared the panic of the people as creatures exploded from the ground, covered in sewage. The creatures howled, slime oozing from their wide toothless mouths. Then, the picture faded to black.

A new song played. The melody was soft and serious but grew sunnier as the screen brightened. The silhouette of a large man standing on a hill came into view. Now the song, like the man, seemed powerful, filling Sunshine with hope. Whoever this man was, holding what appeared to be a mop, he was going to be the one to stand up to the creatures that threatened his world.

Noisy bursts pulled Sunshine's attention away from the screen as the poppers erupted into life. She turned to the Usher-Bot and grinned.

"I liked it!" she said. "Movies are neat. Thank you!"

The Usher-Bot looked at her and then at the screen. "Oh. Oh! My dear human, that was not a movie. That was only a preview. Once your snacks are ready, I'll escort you to the auditorium where you can view the film in its entirety."

Sunshine scrunched her eyebrows. "But I just watched it."

"No, no. That was only bits and pieces of the whole thing. Something to gain the interest of the audience before they see the full story."

"But I already know what happens. The little weirdos come up and wreck stuff. Then, the guy with the mop comes and stops them. I imagine he probably gives them a good whomping for being such jerks."

"Imagine?" Despite the mechanical voice of the robot, it genuinely sounded confused. "You don't need to imagine anything. The film will do that for you."

Sunshine laughed. "Why would I want that?"

The Usher-Bot didn't respond.

"If I watch the whole thing," Sunshine said, "then I don't get to picture in my head what kind of stuff happens. If I let the movie tell me everything, then what's the point of being able to do any of the imagining myself?"

"That is the point. You just relax and let the film tell you what to think. That way, all you need to do is enjoy yourself and indulge in any of our many delicious treats."

With that, the popcorn exploded with full force. Sunshine turned and watched charred seeds shoot from the kettle. While some actually popped into fluffy popcorn, most kernels were long past their shelf life and only burned.

Sunshine looked back at the Usher-Bot. "I don't think I'm gonna be able to eat that. I should probably be going, too. I'm sure Pops and Momsy are wondering where I am."

"But," the Usher-Bot said calmly, "you have to stay."

Sunshine stepped back as tiny popcorn fireballs flew between her and the Usher-Bot. The face on the digital screen of the robot had lost its smile and was now staring blankly at her with a straight, firm line of a mouth.

"I'm gonna go ahead and skip this one," Sunshine said, slowly backing toward the exit. On the other side of the glass door, Barney, the clockwork hare, sat, staring at her.

"Weird," Sunshine said under her breath as she moved toward a different set of doors.

"Just wait right there, young lady," the Usher-Bot said as it moved to block her path. "There's no better fun to have than what we've got here, and we certainly can't let you leave without a smile on your face."

"It's okay. See." Sunshine gave the robot a forced, overly wide grin. "Super happy. Time to go."

She jumped around the robot and ran toward the doors. As her foot landed, she felt herself fall forward. The floor moved, each tile shuffling around, trying to reroute her from her escape to the doors.

Sunshine leaped, trying to gain ground on the moving floor. The Usher-Bot managed to stay right alongside her, the tiles beneath it staying put like tiles should.

Not making any progress, Sunshine jumped to the tile that held the Usher-Bot. With that piece of floor standing still, she was able to move a little closer to the doors.

As she jumped forward, her new tile slid from its place. The Usher-Bot followed, and Sunshine repeated her previous trick, jumping onto its tile to make her way to the door. After doing this three times, she was finally within reach.

Sunshine jumped to the door and reached for the handle. She tugged on the handle and pushed at the door, but it didn't budge.

"Help me!" Sunshine yelled to Barney, who looked back and forth from her to the Usher-Bot.

Then, in a streak of silver, her only hope was gone. Sunshine slumped to the ground in front of the locked door and watched as the tile carried her back into the lobby and the cloud of burning popcorn and flashing chaos of multicolored lights.

The Usher-Bot followed with its digital smile returned to its face-screen.

"You are in for such a treat," the robot said. "Not only do all of our auditoriums feature double cup holders, but today's matinee is a quadruple feature!"

"Great," Sunshine mumbled.

As the tile that carried Sunshine moved around the corner from the concession stand, the rows of multicolored lights ended. The long hallway was dark with the exception of a single spotlight shining far in the distance. Sunshine sat and watched as the Usher-Bot rolled ahead of her into the dark hall until it disappeared.

Sunshine stood up slowly. The tile moved faster, but now with her robot captor gone, she had a chance to make a run for it. Knowing the front doors weren't an option and that Barney was absolutely no help, she looked around. Backlit movie posters seemed to float in the hallway's darkness. As she watched them move by faster and faster, she became unsure of whether she could even jump from the tile without hurting herself. She stopped moving and looked up to see the spotlight in front of her shining down on a star-covered podium where the Usher-Bot now stood.

"Ticket, please," the Usher-Bot said, reaching one of its clawed, metal tentacles toward Sunshine. Sunshine held out the tickets she had got from the Binjo Burger talking horse. The Usher-Bot took both of the tickets, and his smile became impossibly wider.

"Ahh," he said. "A true classic. Unlike our current selection of digital films, this one will be presented in its original 35-millimeter format. The quality may not be as refined as current standards, but we'll just call it 'retro.'"

The Usher-Bot ripped the tickets in half then handed one back to Sunshine and the second to Bunny (that one, of course, fell to ground). Sunshine stuck her ticket stub in her pocket and watched the robot back away. Its metal body seemed to melt into the dark hallway until only the face on its glowing screen could be seen, smiling at her.

"Enjoy the show."

Sunshine stood still, expecting the tile to bring her to her theater, but nothing happened. She heard something moving above her, but when she looked up, couldn't see anything. The grinding noise had come out from somewhere in front of her, moved directly above her head, then stopped. Now, a new noise whistled in its place. Sunshine stared into the shadows until, finally, something shiny lowered from the ceiling.

"Oh, geez," she said, trying to tuck her head between her shoulders.

It looked like one of the metal claws of the Usher-Bot, but this one was much larger.

"Welcome," the claw said, its voice coming from a red light placed between its fingers. "Welcome."

Sunshine groaned as she shrank down. She knew what was about to happen, and she didn't like it.

"Welcome," the claw repeated as it continued to lower itself down to Sunshine.

She tucked Bunny up against her as hard as she could and bent over top of him.

"This place is so creepy," she whispered to the stuffed rabbit.

"Are we having fun yet?" the claw asked in a hollow voice, wrapping its fingers around Sunshine.

Sunshine held Bunny tight, feeling the claw tighten around her. She shivered. "I guess it's movie time."

While music started to play in the distance, Sunshine felt herself jerk; the claw lifted her up.

"Enjoy a complimentary beverage," the claw said. "Bubbly refreshment!"

Sunshine, suspended in air and moving fast, twisted her head around at a new sound coming from above. Another claw lowered and moved alongside hers.

"Bubbly refreshment," the new claw said in a similar, though monotone voice. The second claw held a large paper cup just within Sunshine's reach.

She grabbed the cup, but as she took it, she squeezed too hard, and the lid popped off. Looking inside to see what kind of bubbles and refreshment the theater offered her, she cringed and felt her stomach turn. Inside the cup was a dark-brown sludge that barely moved when she tilted the cup forward.

Sunshine threw down the cup, letting the muck splatter on the floor. She heard another machine whir to life behind her and looked, though now she hung upside-down from the claw's grasp.

"A clean hallway is a happy hallway," the new robot sang, wheeling itself to the discarded cup of sludge. It swept at the cup, a door at its base opened up, and soon the cup disappeared from view.

"A delicious treat to enjoy during your cinematic experience," another voice said. It was the smaller claw, and Sunshine looked up to see it holding out an enormous paper bag. Before she could see inside, the burning stench hit her nose, and she knew it was popcorn.

Sunshine grabbed the bag from the claw to find the blackened, still-smoldering kernels inside. As she was about to throw it to the ground, something inside exploded, and a piece of popcorn shot out at her. Sunshine shielded her eyes with her hands. Then, in horror, she watched as not only the bag, but also Bunny, fell to the ground.

"No, no, no!" Sunshine screamed.

She twisted inside the grip of the claw, trying to escape its clutches, but to no avail. Watching helplessly, her stuffed rabbit sat on the floor beside the spilled popcorn. The sweeper robot was there in a heartbeat to perform its duty.

After making quick work of the popcorn bag, even with the burned kernels spread out everywhere, it turned its attention to Bunny.

"No," Sunshine said. All hope was gone from her voice. "This is definitely not a dream."

The machine's broom swatted Bunny. It paused, then a red light shone from what Sunshine could only call its eye. The light scanned Bunny, the machine twirled around, and a larger door on its backside opened up. Sunshine, still moving fast down the hall, could barely see as the robot consumed her friend.

"Unidentified object," the robot said, still in a singsongy voice. "Reporting to Lost and Found."

The sweeper robot vanished down the dark hallway. Snackless and Bunnyless, Sunshine's heart sank.

The claw holding her jerked and began lowering her to ground. As Sunshine's feet hit the floor, she felt the metal fingers open, and she turned to run after Bunny. But then, she was grabbed once again by steely fingers.

She could tell the grip was different from what had been carrying her before it turned her back to the auditorium door. The Usher-Bot stood above her. The digital face, still smiling, stared down at her.

"No talking during the feature," the robot said. "Do not place your feet on the seats." It pulled her closer to the door. "Please switch your mobile communication devices to silent." The door opened. "Be courteous to the other patrons." The Usher-Bot shoved Sunshine through the doorway. "Crying babies and restless children will be silenced."

Sunshine stumbled forward as the door slammed behind her. Spinning back to it, she pushed the handle, trying to escape the dark hallway. It was locked. She was trapped.

Sunshine turned and leaned her back against the door. Sliding down, she stared into the emptiness of the corridor leading into the auditorium. Alone and scared, seeing a movie was the last thing she wanted to do.

Sunshine closed her eyes and tried to imagine some way out of this. The door was locked. She knew these robots were planning to keep her here forever.

She pictured the hero from the *Muck-Mouths* preview. If only she had a mop.

She thought of the theater rules. She could break them. If she were the worst customer ever, there would be no way they would let her stay.

At the end of the corridor, a dim light glowed. Music started to play. Small lights lining both sides of the floor lit her way.

Sunshine pushed herself off the door. It was time for a show.

# Lost Tomorrow

# Sold-Out Show

Music blared as she looked down the hall and into the dark auditorium. She laughed, envisioning her plan to become the most obnoxious moviegoer this theater had ever seen.

"In a world … " she yelled, making her voice as deep as she could to imitate the narrator, "where a little girl has been kidnapped by crazy robots … " She ran down the corridor. "And where there's nothing to eat except burned-up popcorn and sludge pop. And they stole her Bunny because they wanted her to watch their movies forever … "

Sunshine reached the end of the corridor, crashing into a plastic barricade, and froze. The movie screen was huge, bigger than she could have ever imagined. As gigantic letters flew by, it seemed to open up to a whole other world. Mesmerized, Sunshine shuffled along the seats and watched in silence as the rest of the preview played out.

"It's amazing," Sunshine whispered, staring at giant actors onscreen as they slowly faded. "Coming soon … " she read out loud.

"The show is about to begin," a booming voice said from all around her. The soft light in the theater dimmed further.

Sunshine moved along the aisle, still watching the blank screen, hoping for something new to appear. Bumping into one of the chairs, she glanced down and thought she should find somewhere to sit.

The auditorium was too dark to get a good view, but she could tell it was huge inside. The hundreds of seats went far and wide and up a long flight of stairs. Sunshine made her way up, hoping to find the best view of the screen.

The only light in the auditorium was at the back of the room. Sunshine realized the small bright rectangle was a window. While it didn't emit enough light to reveal anything around her, it felt like a beacon in the darkness.

Sunshine ran up the stairs. Keeping one hand close to the seats, she made her way in the darkness. The odd length of each step and the whirring sound coming from the speakers was disorienting. Sunshine's head spun. Despite knowing she had to escape the theater, all she wanted was to sit down.

Then, she stopped. The projection room window glowed brighter and brighter until it became blinding. Sunshine turned away. Looking back at the screen, the picture came to life.

Almost instantly, she felt transported to another world as the movie images engulfed her. She flew through a clockwork machine. Gears spun, and levers flipped as a mechanical world twisted apart, opened up, and let her see all the inner workings. As she reached the heart of the machine, its yellow core glowed brightly. Letters appeared from nothing, floating center screen.

"Welcome to Academy Cinemas," Sunshine read aloud. "Enjoy the show."

The screen faded to black. The spell was broken, and Sunshine turned away. She closed her eyes and shook her head, trying to get back to the mission at hand. Now was no time to enjoy the show. She needed to escape.

Keeping her back to the screen as music started to play, Sunshine looked up. She felt a chill run down her spine. The light reflecting off the screen filled the auditorium. She should have known she was not alone.

Long ago, this was a nearly sold-out show. Sunshine remembered the vehicles sitting outside. Now she had found their owners. The skeletons, at least the ones whose heads hadn't rolled off, all stared silently up at the screen.

Sunshine tried to ignore the bodies around her and continued her way up the stairway toward the projection room window. Then, a red light shone all around her. She looked back and forth, trying to figure out what happened. The light quickly became brighter, and she realized it came from above her.

"Please, find your seat," a robotic voice said. "The feature is about to begin."

"I'll begin your feature!" Sunshine yelled then shrugged after realizing she didn't know what that meant.

"Please, remain silent," the voice said, sounding closer.

"No."

"Please, do not disturb the other patrons."

"No!" Sunshine shouted. "What are you going to do? Kick me out? To freedom and stuff?"

A beep sounded from above her, and the red light vanished. Sunshine looked around, not sure where it had gone. Then, she smiled.

"That's what I thought."

The film's music grew victorious as the main movie started. Sunshine felt invigorated and skipped up to the next step. There was nothing that robot voice could do to stop—

Something grabbed her from behind, and she instantly recognized the feeling. Like in the hallway leading to the auditorium, the claw tightened around her.

*"Please remain silent!"* it buzzed. *"Please be seated! Please do not disturb the other patrons!"*

Sunshine twisted in its grip and was lifted high into the air. She was carried, as if flying above the audience of the dead, toward the back of the auditorium. Sunshine looked up, blinded by the light from the projector room until she was past the beam. Blinking the spots out of her eyes, she was able to see inside the room. Barney, the silver hare, stared back at her.

"Help!" Sunshine screamed at the robot that had led her to this awful world, trying to be heard over the film's soundtrack.

Barney blinked, twitched his nose, and as usual, did nothing to assist.

"Come on," Sunshine whined as she got even closer.

Soon, she was face to face with him, held just outside the projection room in the grasp of the robot claw.

"They took my Bunny," she said, though she could barely hear her own voice over the blaring music.

Seeing a latch on the other side of the glass, she stretched her hand toward it. But she was being lowered. The claw had found the only open seat in the room.

As the claw released her, Sunshine fell the rest of the way into the chair below, landing between two skeletons.

Looking up from her seat, the light of the projection room was only a sliver. The window was far out of reach, with no visible way to climb the wall in the back row. Sunshine turned, eyes closed, and slumped in her chair.

She knew that if she gave up, if she started to watch the movie, she'd end up just like the rest of the audience. She knew she would never see Bunny again, never find Pops and Momsy, and never get home to Wandering Willows. The skeletons all around her were once people who had real lives, but here they were. They had given in and let the movies take over.

Sunshine tucked her head between her knees and tried to shut out the sound. She tried to think, to come up with some plan to get out of there. As hard as she tried, her mind couldn't focus. All she could hear was *The Return of the Muck-Mouths.*

"The first known incident," a stern-sounding man said, "was years ago. An isolated event in a small elementary school. This one, ladies and gentlemen, will make that day look like a hiccup. From what our data shows, these creatures have been living under the northwestern states for centuries, maybe more. The Wisconsin quarantine seems to have triggered the recent activity, and soon, the full population of this species will surface. If we hesitate to act, the northwestern United States will be lost in twenty-four hours."

There was a chatter throughout the room.

"What are we going to do, Madame President?"

Sunshine, no longer able to resist, opened her eyes and looked up at the screen. The image panned to a woman with sharp features and a scar in the shape of a star running from her nose to her ear and down to her jaw. She stared at the screen, silent.

As she closed her eyes, Sunshine felt her burden. Like Madame President, she faced a problem that was bigger than she knew how to handle. She watched her standing at the head of the table among her advisers. Sunshine saw the stoic focus as she searched her thoughts for a solution. Sunshine knew she had to do the same.

She closed her eyes again, but this time let her mind drift away. She let the images of the dead disappear from her thoughts. She let the memory of robots melt into nothingness. She even let go of the hope she held to return to Wandering Willows. Sunshine cleared her mind of all her fears.

Then, she pictured herself. Sunshine watched as her own image was projected onto a massive movie screen in front of her. Beside the gigantic movie-Sunshine sat Bunny, her own adviser. As Sunshine's mind cast the thoughts of the problems at hand to movie-Sunshine, the imaginary version closed her eyes, stayed calmed, and searched for the answers that Sunshine couldn't find on her own.

Slowly, Sunshine, movie-Sunshine, and Madame President all opened their eyes. They knew what they had to do.

While the scene in the movie played out on the huge screen in front of her, Sunshine ignored it. She looked up, searching for a sign of movement. Though she couldn't see anything, she knew the claw was up there, waiting.

Sunshine sprang from her seat, and as soon as she did, she could hear her captor coming for her. Stepping to the side of the chair she had been assigned, she stood in front of her skeleton neighbor.

"Sorry," Sunshine said as she took it by the fleshless hand. "I'm gonna need your help."

She pulled the skeleton away from its seat. Tugging too hard, Sunshine caused the entire arm to come loose.

"Sorry again!"

Grabbing the other arm, Sunshine pulled, trying to keep a firm grip while not ripping the arm free. She heard the claw lowering itself from the ceiling.

"Hurry," she whispered to herself.

She lifted the body most of the way off of the seat. Draping the rattling bones onto her head and shoulders, it was only a moment before she felt the weight lifted up off of her. The claw had it.

She watched as the skeleton rose up above her. It moved just to the right and stopped. The claw opened and slinked back into the shadows, and the skeleton fell into the seat she had previously been sitting in.

"It worked!" Sunshine cheered.

Stepping over to her old seat, Sunshine pulled the skeleton down and pushed it to the next seat over.

"Back out of my seat, ya goon!" Sunshine yelled.

She moved down the aisle to the next skeleton, grabbed it and pulled it over the top of her, and waited until the claw came to do its job. Sunshine snuck after the flying robot back to her original chair, waited for the skeleton to drop, and shoved it onto the first one.

Sunshine ran back and forth, continuing to build her pile. Soon, she would have a huge stack of skeletons.

"This is it," someone said.

Startled by the voice, Sunshine turned around. She had forgotten all about *The Return of the Muck-Mouths*. On the screen, a man with thick glasses spoke to a weird-looking creature with pale-green skin and eyes too big for its head.

"This is our last chance," the man said. "You are our last chance. If we don't quarantine this region, not only will all of the United States be in danger, but perhaps the entire world.

"Don't panic, my friend," the creature said. "This is our specialty."

Sunshine looked up at the mountain of the dead and smiled. At the top was her path to freedom.

Sunshine climbed slow and steady. Bones crunched beneath her feet as she struggled to keep her balance. Surprisingly, the pile held firm. Sunshine looked down at the skeleton she had left in her chair to keep the claw from returning.

"Thanks, buddy," she whispered, hoping the flying, clawed robots wouldn't notice what happened.

Sunshine stretched up to the window of the projection room. She could hear the hum of the machines inside. Peeking through the glass, she watched Barney dart back and forth as he worked.

*Tap, tap, tap.*

Barney stopped. He looked at the window and, twitching his black nose, tilted his head. Sunshine waved. He was so fast that she couldn't see him move toward her, but they were now face to face.

Sunshine smiled and pointed to the window latch. Barney looked up to it, back to her, then over his shoulder as if to make sure no one was watching. He hopped and slapped the latch open with his paw.

Pressing her palms against the thick glass, Sunshine slid the window open. The hushed sound of the projector became a roar, and she could see more than a dozen wheels spinning behind a glass door on the machine, guiding the film through it. Sunshine grabbed onto the edge of the window frame and pulled herself up. Heaving herself through the window, she tumbled to the floor.

Back on her feet, Sunshine looked in awe at the machines around her as they chirped, their motors whirring. Next to the projector, a big plastic cart was tipped on its side. Rolls of unwound film trailed out from the cart like spilled noodles.

As Sunshine walked toward Barney, she heard something. Turning, she saw a radio clutched between two skeletal hands belonging to someone wearing the same checkered suspenders and bowtie as the Usher-Bot and the silver hare.

"Okay, you," she said, turning from the body and walking away from the noise of the projector. "You led me here. Now I need your help to get back home. Did you know this place was full of crazies?"

The robot, like her own Bunny, returned a blank stare.

"Don't look at me like that. You know where we are. You know how to get us out of here."

Still silent.

Sunshine pinched the bridge of her nose and closed her eyes. "This escape plan is not going as planned."

Taking a deep breath, Sunshine tried to focus, to block out the projection room noise and figure out some way to deal with the situation. She thought about everything she had to work with, which unfortunately wasn't much. Then she remembered the machines in the projection booth.

Sunshine opened her eyes. This world was different from hers, but everything seemed to have its place and work together in one way or another. She knew what to do.

"This way," Sunshine said to Barney as she ran back to the noisier end of the room.

Sunshine grabbed the cart. Rolls of film tumbled aside, unwinding like ribbons as she took off. Down a little ways from the projector, she skidded to a stop and spun around. Eyeing the machine, Sunshine snickered.

She stared at it. She had no idea how the projector worked, how it made the pictures on the rolls of film into the movies on the big screen. How it pulled the film in one end, wound it through all the weird gears and wheels, then managed to roll it back together on the other side without causing a giant mess.

Then, she laughed again. Knowing how the machine worked didn't matter. She knew that it worked. And for some reason, she knew that parts inside it would work for what she wanted, though she wasn't even sure what that was. Whether she was back home helping Pops tinker or giving Momsy a hand with one of her art projects, Sunshine had a gift for figuring out things she had no reason to understand. Working with this machine would be no different.

 She aimed the metal cart straight toward the control panel of the machine. Then, running full speed, she could hear herself laughing like a maniac.

Holding tight to the handle as the cart collided with the projector, Sunshine was in a daze. Dials and buttons flew everywhere. She bashed the cart into the projector over and over, breaking off the metal paneling that protected the insides of the machine.

When the mechanical guts spilled across the floor, Sunshine finally paused and felt a cool calm come over her. With Barney standing still, staring at her with unblinking eyes, a grin stretched across her face.

"Jump up here," Sunshine said, pointing at the top of the cart.

He did, and Sunshine dug through the insides of the projector. She ripped out a handful of blue wires and flung them up to the cart. The silver hare sniffed at them then swatted them away with his paw. Sunshine noticed and smiled. She pulled out another handful, gave them to the robot to inspect, and he shook his head. Groaning, Sunshine looked farther back into the machine. Seeing a thicker black cable, she tugged at it.

"This one? It's this one, isn't it?"

Barney nodded.

"Okey dokey," Sunshine said, ripping the cable out of the projector.

She tossed it to Barney and ran around the cart to the remains of the former human projectionist.

"Need to borrow this," Sunshine said as she grabbed the dead man's radio and yanked the cord from the wall. Then, spotting a small rusty toolbox beside the skeleton, she smiled.

"That, too."

Barney hopped aside as Sunshine threw the radio and the toolbox on top of the cart. Flicking the latches, she opened the toolbox. Her grin grew even wider when she found a drill just like the one Pops had. Drill in hand, she pulled the trigger. Despite all odds, the bit spun to life.

Laughter echoed through the projector room corridor. The silver hare watched in silence as the girl cackled, hard at work, tearing into the electronics of the radio and searching for all the right pieces.

Sunshine eyed the robot. "You're onto what we're doing, aren't you?"

Barney climbed on top of the cart, and his white eyes flashed then became green. He nudged the speaker from the disassembled radio. Pulling his right ear like a lever, a panel on top of his head opened to reveal a small cavity. Sunshine's eyes narrowed as she grinned.

Sunshine examined the speaker and the hole in the robot's skull. With a few minor adjustments, a little bit of drilling, and some cramming of this into that, the speaker was set in place.

"*Bzzzt* Hello."

"You can talk! Oh, my gosh! Oh, my gosh! I'm Sunshine! What's your name? It probably isn't Barney, I suppose. I just needed something to call you, so sorry to have to make something up. Why are here? What's the deal with that crazy Usher-Bot? Do you know how to get out of here? We should get of here! How long have you been here? Why'd you even bring me? Why didn't you just stay in the swamp? It's pretty nice there, and if you lived there, I could probably talk Pops and Momsy into having more picnics. It was my first time in Ballihag, but since I'm older now, they'll probably take me more. Maybe not though, since I got lost and ended up here, but if you help me get back, maybe they'll be okay with having more picnics. I like picnics! We brought—"

"First things first," the silver hare said as it stood up tall, just as tall as Sunshine. "My name *is* Barney."

"Barney! You like the name I made up for you!"

He turned away and peered down the hallway. "Coincidence, actually. We should be on our way. Intermission is almost upon us."

Sunshine followed Barney down the dark hall, away from the theater where *The Return of the Muck-Mouths* could still be heard. She rushed up and grabbed the robot by its arm.

"Wait! Before we go, I need your help. I need to find Bunny."

"Bunny? Your toy mockery of rabbit-kind?"

"Hey! You're not exactly a real rabbit, either."

"No. We are already running late. If Intermission begins before we can get out of here, I fear all hope is lost."

"Geez, Louise. We're just going to be late for lunch. It's not like the end of the world or anything. And even if it was, then I'd want Bunny with me. The sweeper robot said it was taking him to Lost and Found."

The robot buzzed. "It's on our way. We'll find your Bunny. But we must hurry."

# Lost Tomorrow

# Lost and Found

Blue light emitted from Barney's eyes, guiding the two through the projection room corridor. Sunshine, unable to see very far in the dim glow, collided with the metal back of the clockwork hare when it stopped walking.

"There," Barney said quietly with the volume of his voice turned down. "The way to Lost and Found."

There was a hatch in the floor. The wheel to open it, rusted from ages of neglect, looked as though it would be impossible to budge. Pulling her sleeves over her hands, Sunshine gripped the wheel and gave it a tug. Nothing happened.

"Well," she said. "Guess we'll have to go all tough guy on this."

Sunshine stepped back and rolled up her sleeves.

"Here we go!"

Sunshine pounced on the wheel, grabbing it tight with both hands. With a determined jerk, she felt it move. Then, she fell. The wheel was now in her hands, no longer attached to the hatch.

"Oops."

Barney shook his head and walked to the hatch. Getting down on all fours, he examined it.

"What are we going to do?" Sunshine asked.

"Hold this," Barney said, raising his paw to Sunshine.

Confused, Sunshine took it in her hands. Then, sparks ringed his wrist, making a bracelet of light. The robot's paw disconnected and fell loose in her hands.

"Careful," Barney said. "Might be hot."

Something new emerged from the arm of the robot, and Sunshine recognized the whir of a drill. Barney lowered his drill-paw into the hole where the hatch's wheel used to sit. While rust and dust and sparks flew into the air, Sunshine covered her face until she heard something snap.

Barney stepped back from the hatch. The drill slid back into his arm, and Sunshine handed him the paw, which he quickly reattached. Then, Barney reached down to the hatch and pried it open.

The door in the floor opened, and Sunshine excitedly peered into what appeared to be a ventilation shaft. Though she had no idea what could be waiting, she was eager to move on with her search for Bunny.

"Wait," Barney said as Sunshine grabbed hold of the ladder. "It'll be dark down there."

The robot leaned forward. The blue light in his right eye changed to green and shone even brighter. Three clicks came from the robot's head, and then, the glowing eyeball popped out. Sunshine caught it out of reflex.

She grimaced. "You're kind of gross."

"Hurry along."

Sunshine climbed down, trying to keep a grip on the eyeball. As she reached the bottom, she moved into the narrow ventilation shaft and listened as Barney followed her. Using her light, she looked down the only two paths she could take but saw no clue as to which one to take. At random, she chose to go right, and soon the robot followed.

After a short while Barney said, "Stop here."

Sunshine twisted around to look over her shoulder at the robot. She held up the eyeball to see that he had both paws against the wall, tapping various locations.

"I know a shortcut."

Barney's body contorted. His head extended out from his body as his neck grew longer. Then, his neck bent in a way that would leave any person broken. Now his head, perfectly upright and looking at the wall, trembled. He produced a whining sound that worked its way up his throat until his mouth opened and his jaw unhinged.

A head, tiny compared to Barney's but still with the long ears and dark-gray patch over one eye, emerged from his throat. Its tiny mouth opened and unhinged just like Barney's original had.

"Please don't have another creepy rabbit head in there," Sunshine pleaded.

A blue laser light shot out from the mini-Barney's mouth. Barney's regular-sized head guided the laser and cut a rectangular hole, leaving the edges glowing with molten metal.

As the cut was finished, the little rabbit head let out a cheer and wriggled its way back down Barney's throat. Then, reaching up with one paw, Barney punched, and the metal piece of wall flew out of sight. Light from the room beyond filled the ventilation shaft.

Sunshine followed Barney through the hole. Before seeing what was inside the room, a horrid smell hit her. The theater's trash compactor hadn't been emptied for a very, very long time.

Luckily, some of the soda cups, popcorn bags, and candy wrappers created enough of an intact pile to climb down from the ventilation shaft. As Sunshine slid down, Barney stopped her from going too far and into the waste that wasn't so intact. Decomposition had turned much of the garbage into a black tar that pooled in the bottom of the compactor. Sunshine could only wonder how deep it went.

"We have to hurry," Barney said, returning his glowing eyeball to its place. "Intermission is coming."

"I don't know what that means," Sunshine said, trying to cling onto the robot's back to keep from dipping her toes in the muck.

"It means that all of what you see here is due for compaction. The janitorial staff is scheduled, no matter the attendance of any film, to clear waste from the building immediately following Intermission and deposit it here. Before they can, the volume of the existing refuse must be minimized."

Sunshine looked around. "You mean squished, don't you?"

"Correct."

"Well," Sunshine said, "we better … "

A sudden rumbling began; the walls started to vibrate. It was only a moment before they started to do their job and move inward.

"That seems about right," Sunshine muttered, glaring at the walls.

"This way," Barney said, shuffling through the trash. His legs lengthened, keeping himself and Sunshine above the tar pit of filth.

Sunshine felt Barney's paws reach around and pull her off of his back. He spun his head in a half circle until he faced her.

"Hang on."

Sunshine held tight to Barney's wrists as his arms extended out from his body farther than she would have imagined possible. As he lifted her well above the garbage, she turned to see a small doorway set high in the one wall that was still stationary. Below her, she could see the trash on the floor rising as the side walls slowly moved toward one another. Soon, everything inside would be crushed.

Reaching the doorway, Sunshine climbed from Barney's paws and into the small hole. Once used to let garbage slide down, the slanted metal pocket was just big enough for Sunshine to sit inside. Looking around the door for something to grab onto, she found nothing. She braced herself against the walls of the hole with her feet and back and tried to push the door open. It didn't budge.

"I can't open it!" she yelled.

"The door folds in," Barney said, his voice volume turned all the way up to be heard over the sound of the moving walls. His arms were now extended from side to side to keep the walls from moving closer. Though they were still closing in, they appeared to be shaking from Barney's resistance.

"Try prying it open from the bottom."

Sunshine did as he said, but her fingers, as tiny as they were, couldn't fit under the edge of the steel door. Even if they could, Sunshine doubted she had the strength to lift the heavy metal.

"Can't get it!" Sunshine shouted over the garbage folding in on itself.

Barney looked back and forth at the walls. The shaking grew more and more violent as the compactor tried to do its job. Sunshine watched him, knowing that if he were to move to try and help her, the robot would lose his grip and be crushed along with the trash and sludge around him. But without a way to open the door, once the walls closed in, she would be trapped in the tiny garbage chute.

Sunshine squeezed her eyes shut. The noisy compactor's gears and the sound of discarded concessions being smashed filled her ears. She tried to clear her head, tried to think of some way out of this mess. If she couldn't, she would be stuck and her friend would be destroyed.

Then, silence.

Sunshine opened her eyes. Instead of the compactor's noise, she could hear the hums and beeps of Barney's robot body as he worked to delay his inevitable doom. Somehow, she could feel the current of electricity inside him as his inner workings attempted to use their programming to find a solution to his dilemma. She smelled the sticky filth rising up beneath her from the floor of the compactor and could taste the rot in her mouth. And then, Sunshine found what she was looking for.

"Barney!" she yelled. "Use your weird, little mouth-face!"

"What?"

"That mini-rabbit head in your mouth! Bring it out, and stick it in the slime. Then, get it up here."

Barney opened his mouth, and the little face extended from his throat. Sunshine thought she heard the robot gag as the mini-face dipped into the sludge.

"Good! Now, up here."

The throat-face thing extended out, quickly arriving at Sunshine. She cringed as the smell of the muck hit her nose. Covering her face, she pointed at bottom of the door.

"Use the sticky," she said in a muffled voice beneath her hand.

The little face smacked into the bottom of the door. Sunshine looked to make sure it was in place then waved back to Barney's normal-sized head.

"Nice and easy. Pull the door back."

The sludge held, and as soon as the crack beneath the door widened enough, Sunshine grabbed it and pulled. Ducking to make room, she held the door open.

"Get up here!" she yelled to Barney.

The robot's arms were shaking. The walls of the compactor were only a few feet apart from each other, with Barney trapped between them.

"Negative," the robot responded. "It will be impossible for me to reach you."

"You have to! I need your help!"

"You'll have it."

Sunshine heard a snap and watched in terror as the walls moved in. Fortunately, the snapping sound wasn't from Barney's arms finally breaking free, but was the weird throat rabbit protruding from his mouth. From corner of her eye, she saw the mechanical critter fall.

Catching itself on the slanted floor, it flopped around like a fish, spattering the black tar everywhere. Sparks emitted from the extension, just as they had done when Barney removed his paw.

The rabbit-faced, tadpole-like chunk of robot grew arms and legs. It hopped up to its feet and looked at Sunshine.

"Let's go," it said in a high-pitched voice.

"But … "

"Don't worry about that," the new robot said, glancing down at the rest of his body. "It's only a shell."

The tiny metal robot leaped through the doorway and into the hall. Sunshine looked back just in time to see the rest of Barney— the clockwork hare she had followed here, the one who tried to help her escape—being crushed between the walls of the trash compactor.

Climbing up the garbage chute and into the hall, Sunshine felt a cold chill throughout her whole body. Although she had spent a lot of her day fumbling around with skeletons, to see something so awful happen to someone she knew was something she wasn't ready for. She looked at the new robot in front of her, unsure what to say.

"I am still Barney," the little robot said. "The programming that you know as Barney is just as much a part of me as it was him. And as soon as I find something to eat, you won't even notice the difference."

"Robots eat?"

"Something like that. Now, come this way."

Sunshine followed the robot's lead. Not far down the hall, a backlit sign above a plain green door.

The sign read, "Lost and Found."

# Lost and Found

Sunshine turned the handle and cracked open the door. Before there was enough space for her to peek in, the tiny robot slid inside for a first look. Sunshine waited for only a moment before the robot returned. He signaled Sunshine to follow.

Seeing a long flight of stairs leading into the dim light, Sunshine slowly walked into the Lost and Found. Bigger than she would have guessed from the size of the door, the room must have stretched throughout the entire basement. Massive stacks filled the room. It was as though people used to come to the theater just to lose their personal effects.

"We're never gonna find him in here," Sunshine groaned.

The robot darted back and forth, up and down the piles closest to the entrance. Though fast, the miniature version of Barney didn't move with the flurry of speed his previous body had.

"We can make this go a bit faster," the robot said, standing on top of a pile dedicated to sunglasses.

"Okey dokey," Sunshine said. "How can I help?"

"We need to find cellular phones."

"Okay. What's that?"

"Portable communication devices. Generally rectangular. Should fit in your hand. Computers would work, as well. However, we should start small."

"All righty," Sunshine said.

Sunshine ran deeper into Lost and Found, only half looking for the phones. What she really longed for had to be here.

"Buuuuunnnny!" Sunshine yelled.

Of course, there was never a reply.

Lost and Found seemed to go on forever, filled with piles of jackets, toys, purses and backpacks, kids' clothes, and an illogical amount of shoes. She wondered what people had left to wear after leaving the movies. Soon, Sunshine had no idea where she was or how far she'd come.

As she ran between another pair of junk heaps, her toe caught on something, and her body flew forward.

"D'oh," Sunshine said, bracing herself for impact.

Hitting with a sharp thud, Sunshine skidded across the floor. Shaking her head and brushing the dust off, she picked herself up and looked for the thing that had tripped her.

A small, dark animal stood staring at her.

"Hello?" Sunshine watched the creature, unsure of whether she should try to talk to it or turn around and start running full speed.

It remained quiet and unmoving. Sunshine stepped closer. Most of its body was furry and black with the exception of a seemingly misplaced strip of white on its back.

"What are you?"

With each step forward, Sunshine felt unease twisting in the pit of her stomach. The animal seemed to be glaring at her. Between its cold, dead eyes was a weird long nose like what she had seen on drawings of elephants. But this was no elephant.

As Sunshine stepped closer, the animal remained still. She stood up tall, looking down at it. No response. Whatever this was, it was not a threat.

Sunshine walked up and tapped the thing with her foot. It felt familiar. Picking it up, she realized the trunk-nosed animal was just a toy—a stuffed animal like Bunny.

The mopey-faced creature had a small white tag hanging off one of the back legs.

"Dave the Tapir," Sunshine read.

"What's that?" a familiar voice asked through the sound of chewing.

Sunshine turned to see Barney. It was not the tiny critter that had sprouted from her robot friend's throat, but the silver hare that had led her into this whole mess. He appeared to be even larger than he was the last time she saw him. Holding a keyboard that was missing a large chunk from it, the robot continued to chew.

"How are you here?"

"What do you mean?" the robot asked with wires hanging out of his mouth like noodles.

"I mean," Sunshine said, "you're you again. You're back to being Barney. And I think you've gotten bigger."

Barney looked down at himself. "Well, yes. Yes, I have. However, I'm not the Barney you may think I am. I can very much assure you that one was destroyed."

Sunshine scrunched up her face. "I'm confused."

The silver hare held up the remaining chunk of keyboard. "Electronics. I found a stack of items, some of which I have no idea why anyone would bring to a film. I figured I would be more useful to you if I would return to the size of my previous body, so I consumed enough to grow." He belched. "May have eaten a little too much."

"Oh," Sunshine said, nodding. "You get big quick."

"Quite right."

Sunshine turned back to the stuffed tapir, Dave. Knowing that Lost and Found did have some sort of organization to it, she looked around to see where he'd come from.

"Can I get a little more light here?" she asked the robot.

Barney's eyes lit up, casting a bright light onto the piles of miscellanea all around them. Sunshine smiled when she saw exactly what she hoped for.

Running up to the huge stack of stuffed toys, she looked around for Bunny. Not seeing him anywhere, she jumped on top of the pile.

"Up we go!" Sunshine cheered as she landed halfway up the mess, still holding the sad-looking tapir.

The soft toys squeaked and squished as she tried to climb. Although she struggled to make her way up, she soon felt the floor beneath her feet again and realized she had made no progress to begin with. Tucking Dave under her arm, Sunshine pulled the stuffed animals down from the pile and tossed them aside.

"No need for that," Barney said.

Sunshine turned to see Barney standing above her. His long ears stood straight up then flattened sideways and started to spin.

Sunshine's hair blew back from the wind. He lifted up off the ground and hovered above her. Sunshine braced herself.

Barney's hind legs hooked under her arms, and her feet left the ground. Rising higher and higher, they arrived at the top of the pile in only a moment.

"Bunny! He's right there!" Sunshine yelled over the whopwhop-whop of the robo-copter blades.

Barney lowered Sunshine to the top of pile. Trying to keep from sinking into the stuffed animals, Sunshine crawled over to Bunny and grabbed him.

"Hey, buddy," she said, squeezing the stuffed rabbit. "We're getting out of here."

Sunshine looked at Dave the Tapir in her arms next to Bunny. The sad glass eyes stared back at her, full of despair.

"Don't look at me like that," Sunshine said. "I'll put you right up top here. You can be the king of lost toys."

Sunshine felt a little bit of her heart shrink as she set Dave on top of the pile. Though it was only a toy, the long-nosed face seemed full of hopelessness, knowing it was doomed to be left behind to spend eternity in the Lost and Found.

As Sunshine slowly backed away from the solemn tapir, she heard something. Somewhere, music played. Looking up to Barney, who continued to hover, she saw his eyes glow brighter. His head spun around to scan the room. Rapid beeps rang out from the robot, keeping rhythm with the crescendoing music from outside the massive Lost and Found.

Sunshine listened to the lyrics of the song, trying to make out what they were saying. Then, clearly hearing the words, she turned to Barney. Wrinkling her eyebrows, she said the lyrics aloud.

"Let's all go to the lobby?"

# Intermission

"Are you ready?"

Sunshine nodded.

"Good." Barney took hold of Sunshine again with his hind legs. He flew so fast that the piles below her were indistinguishable. Soon, they were back to the Lost and Found entrance.

Barney dropped Sunshine quickly, but gently, so she only had a slight stumble before regaining her balance.

"Stay quiet," the robot said, his voice barely audible.

The music, now that they were near the hallway, seemed to be getting louder. Sunshine tiptoed to the door and pushed it open as slowly and quietly as she could and peeked out. Small amber lights flashed up and down the hallway. Barney didn't need to tell her what was happening. Sunshine knew the thing he'd been worrying about had arrived. This was Intermission.

"We have to hurry," Barney said. "The Concessionaughts are coming. At the end of this hall, we should find an emergency exit."

"Concessionaughts? Well, those definitely sound like an emergency."

"You have no idea how right you are."

Barney stepped into the hall and signaled Sunshine to follow. In the distance, she could see large silhouettes of some new creatures bouncing and fumbling their way forward. In the opposite direction, glowing amber letters spelled out "EXIT."

Barney pulled Sunshine back by the shoulder, but she stayed still, watching the menacing figures moving closer.

"Let's all go to the lobby," they sang in shrill, monotone voices.

"What do they want?" Sunshine asked, her voice trembling.

Barney continued to pull at her. "For you to get yourself a treat. All the treats. Forever."

Sunshine broke her gaze from creatures lumbering toward them.

"Forever? But I need to get back home."

"Don't worry. I know a way."

Sunshine turned to follow Barney, who ran, but not so fast as to leave her behind. The music followed them, growing even louder.

Sunshine tripped, catching hold of Barney before falling to her knees. Glancing back, the Concessionaughts were gaining ground. It made her want to run faster than she ever had.

The things were gigantic, nearly as tall as the ceiling. As they moved through the halls, their limbs twitched in a way that made no sense. Their faces were frozen in place and looked like cartoons, just like the Binjo Burger horse or the picture on her movie ticket. And though their mouths didn't move, they kept on singing.

The closest one looked like a giant candy bar with chocolatey goo oozing out of its eyes. The second robot resembled a popcorn box, same as the ones she had seen when first arriving in the theater, but much, much larger. Popcorn kernels, too big to be real, spilled everywhere as the robot spasmed forward. Bringing up the rear of the concession procession was a red-and-white striped soda cup. Luckily, the beverage itself was fake, solid to keep from slushing out everywhere. The cup, missing one of its legs, dragged its bottom half across the floor, limbs flailing to keep pace with the other animatronic monstrosities.

"Let's all go to the lobby … "

Sunshine clutched Bunny and kept running after Barney. Everything felt like a blur as the chipper song rang out all around her and the lights in the hallway flashed against the walls. Then, the hall opened up to a larger area. In it was a concession stand, smaller than the one in the lobby, but still with burning fireballs of popcorn erupting from a kettle.

"Large soda! Only ten dollars more!" a robot behind the stand screeched on autopilot, as it wasn't necessarily directing the deal toward Sunshine or Barney.

"Come on," Barney said, running up to the stand.

Sunshine kept an eye on the robot server as Barney picked her up and lifted her onto the counter.

"Through the scullery," he said pointing to a narrow space leading behind the concession stand.

Sunshine climbed down from the counter just as Barney hopped on top of it. She peeked into the back kitchen area where everything was dark.

"I need one of your eyeballs!" Sunshine shouted.

As she turned back to Barney, she saw that the Concessionaughts had reached them. She cringed, hearing the snapping and slapping of their arms thrashing against themselves, the counters, and each other.

"Let's all go to the lobby!"

Sunshine, no longer willing to wait for Barney to hand her one of his glowing eyeballs, ran into the darkness of the scullery. She held out one hand to guide her. Feeling nothing, she stepped carefully. The floor felt spongy under her feet.

Pressing on, her hand came up against something squishy coated in a sticky film. She felt faint. After a day of seeing monster robots and rooms full of skeletons, Sunshine was sure the slimy tendril in her hand was part of something awful. As she squeezed it, the thick slushing sound made her cringe.

"This way," Barney said, his eyes now lighting up the scullery.

Sunshine blinked to better see what oddity her hand had come up against. She let out a deep breath, seeing a rack of boxed bags of liquid with the Binjo name, the same as the burger restaurant.

Sunshine turned away from the rack and ran after Barney. The kitchen was long and narrow and full of sharp turns through which only robot workers would be able to maneuver comfortably. After every turn in the hallway-like scullery, Sunshine crashed into a wall before bouncing off to regain her footing and head in a new direction. Finally, Sunshine saw the food service area open up wide. However, she was right back where she started, but now on the servers' side of the counter in the main lobby.

"We can't," Sunshine said in a fast and hushed voice. "The doors are all locked."

"That's okay," Barney said, lifting Sunshine onto the countertop. "We'll get through them."

"But … "

He climbed up beside her and then stood still. His face, his chest, and limbs separated just like his old body had done with his jaw to let the strange little rabbit face out of his mouth. A chilly blue light glowed, and mist puffed out from his joints like breath in winter.

"What's happening?"

Sunshine stepped forward, watching the robot's outer casing spread wider and rise up toward her. Sunshine's foot slipped. Her arms flailed as she tried to catch her balance. Then, before she could fall off the concession counter, the robot grabbed her and pulled her into his still-expanding coverings.

She felt the cold metal of Barney's shell wrap around her. It started with her arms, folding around them like the shiny sleeves of a shirt put on wrong. Next, it closed in around her chest while the arms expanded, spreading over the backs of her hands. Trying to keep hold of Bunny, Sunshine tossed him from hand to hand as the metal shell formed gloves.

Something braced the back of Sunshine's head, and though it didn't seem to hold too tight, she couldn't shake free. Sunshine's head jerked forward.

"Ouch," she said.

"Sorry."

She watched Barney's head, the inside of it, lower over her face like a snow mask without eyeholes.

"What's happening?" she asked again.

The last puffs of mist left the shell and, along with them, the blue light. Sunshine was now helpless, enclosed in Barney's body.

She couldn't see out. Everything was dark and quiet. There were no more explosions of popcorn or "Let's all go to the lobby." There was only the sound of her own breath.

"Are you ready?" asked a hollow voice

Sunshine tried to look around but still couldn't move.

"Barney?"

The blue light returned and changed to green, filling the robot shell and forcing Sunshine to close her eyes. Blinking them open and closed, she quickly grew accustomed to the light and could see what was happening. She could see everything now, the entire lobby.

She could see even better from inside Barney than she could before. The areas too dim to see were now illuminated. Looking across the room at the entranceway, each door was highlighted, and glowing letters floated next to them indicating they were potential exits.

Sunshine felt herself slump. Realizing she could now move, she stood up tall. She held up her metal-encased hands, and Bunny looked back at her. As she tossed him from one hand to the other once again, she knew that it was her turn to drive.

Sunshine whipped toward the concession stand. The robot servers all stared at her, quiet, probably not sure who this new robot was. The popcorn burst from the machines, and Sunshine discovered that her Barney eyes could let her watch in slow motion and even zoom in and out as each kernel flew through the air.

"Barney," Sunshine said, "let's go home."

A map appeared before her eyes, marking her current location. She also saw a large X and a path showing how to get there. The X seemed far away, too far. Sunshine tilted her head trying to get a different view of the map. Somehow, it worked, giving her a three-dimensional view. She could see over and under and all the way through the underground city. The place Barney directing her to was deep, farther from the direction she wanted to go.

"But Barney, we need to go up. Back to the Bog. Back to Wandering Willows."

"Negative. You can't return the way you came." He took back control for a moment and turned her in the direction he wanted them to take.

Wanting to run back to the pit that she first fell through to reach the underground city, she tried to keep control of the robot body. As she imagined herself running home as fast as she could, different screens popped up in her vision within the helmet. Words and pictures flashed before her. Though she could read some of it, parts were in languages and symbols she didn't recognize.

"I need to go up. I need to get back home." Sunshine felt the robot's body pulling against her.

"Not yet. First, I need your help."

"That's crazy talk!" Sunshine yelled. "We can't go down to get back up!"

"I need you to trust me," Barney's voice assured her.

"I … I just want to go back home."

Sunshine felt herself jerk forward. Then, imagining herself jumping down from the concession counter, she did exactly that. She had taken control of Barney's metal shell.

"Please," Barney said.

Suddenly, there was an explosion behind Sunshine. Something had burst through the back wall. She ducked as one of the popcorn kettles flew past her and across the lobby. The concession stand was engulfed in a cloud of smoke and dust.

"You cannot leave!" a voice screeched.

As debris from the shattered wall and popcorn machine settled, the Usher-Bot was there. The robot's arms flailed, smacking against the soda machines and automated vendors who were still rambling on about what a great deal they had on large sodas.

"You must stay for the matinee!"

"You're a matinee!" Sunshine yelled.

She spun around and faced the glass doors on the other side of the lobby. Just as she imagined herself running straight through them, a display popped up inside the helmet. She focused on a number by a dial labeled "Accelerator." Using her mind to crank up the dial, the number rapidly increased to triple digits. Then, looking at a green glowing button beside it that read "GO," Sunshine blinked.

The world around her turned to a blur as she hurtled forward.

"Ugh!" She felt herself whipped backward by the grasp of a mechanical tentacle wrapped around her leg.

"Let me go!"

"If you do not stay," the Usher-Bot said, "who will watch our movies?"

The lights inside the helmet flashed. "You have to give me control," Barney said, his voice filling her ears.

"Who will eat our delicious and nutritious snacks?" the Usher-Bot asked, tilting his head innocently.

"I need your help," Barney pleaded.

"Who will be here to have the best time ever?"

"We need to stop this, once and for all."

"Who will we serve forever?"

"This city needs to know it is dead."

Sunshine struggled, trying to pull free from the Usher-Bot. Though she still felt in control over her new robot body, she was helpless in the grip of the Usher-Bot. Its tentacle arm pulled hard, and Sunshine fell to the ground. Before she had a chance to pick herself up, she whipped into the air. Hanging upside down, she came face to face with the Usher-Bot.

The Usher-Bot's features were distorted by static flashes, going from the smile it had worn when she first met it to a look of rage. A panel on its belly opened, and another metal arm jutted out.

Unlike the tentacle arms with the small grabbing fingers, this new one ended with a spinning saw blade.

The saw moved closer to Sunshine, but like much of the machinery she'd seen in the theater, this one was old and worn. The blade, loose in its mount, shook from side to side while the gears smoked and sparks flew in every direction. As she hung helplessly, watching the blade move closer, she could still feel Barney fighting her for control of his body.

She closed her eyes and did her best to forget she was inside a robot's metal armor. She imagined she was back home in Wandering Willows, sitting under a tree with Bunny and knowing nothing about this crazy robot world. Then, she felt Barney's body twist.

A flurry of metal against metal erupted in front of her. Her connection with Barney was broken, and the robot was back in control of his body. Sunshine watched the robots clash just outside her armor. She could feel something warm around her chest as light spun circles in her vision. Then, with a sound like thunder, a silver flare burst from Barney's chest, blasting into the Usher-Bot and sending it flying through the back wall of the concession stand.

Sunshine and Barney fell to the ground, but with the clockwork hare back in control, they were soon on their feet.

"I need your help," Barney said, his voice rapid but calm. "I need you. We need to make things right."

Sunshine tried to shake her head inside the robot. "But can't I just leave? Can't you guys just hang out here and watch the movies without having any people around?"

"It is our duty to serve. You are not the only one who has fallen into this world and been trapped. I can't allow that to happen again, so I led you here because I need you to pull the plug that should have been pulled ages ago. I need you to bring an end to this world once and for all."

"That just … it just seems kinda mean. I'm not the kind of kid that goes around ending worlds."

"You will be. This world ended long ago. You'll be saving the lives of anyone who arrives in this city in the future."

Sunshine stayed quiet. She wanted to take control of the robot's body and run, run straight up the walls of the underground city and crash through the ceiling that locked out her world. She imagined herself back home, back to playing adventure with Bunny in Wandering Willows. But she knew if anyone were to wander into the Ballihag Bog and end up here, they would join the skeletons that filled the cinema.

Sunshine closed her eyes, gave up any remaining control, and let Barney lead the way.

# Lost Tomorrow

# The Big Picture

Instantly, they were running at full speed.

Deeper in the city, buildings lining each block seemed to be standing only by sheer luck. Entire floors were missing. Walls had crumbled. Some areas were black from long-ago fires, while others were just piles of rubble. One road was lined with the statues of men and women, but almost every one had been knocked from its pedestal and was lying broken on the ground.

They sped closer to a large complex of buildings in the distance that were surrounded by a tall, barbed wire fence. Ready to crash into it, Sunshine did what she could to brace herself, though that wasn't much inside the rigid frame of the robot body.

Sunshine heard a hiss and felt a familiar warmth against her chest. Barney's arms spread wide without stopping their charge toward the fence. Then, a beam of light shot forward and instantly melted a huge hole to clear the way.

The main building was a massive dome with smooth concrete walls unlike many of the block-shaped buildings in the compound. The smaller buildings were all made of metal, covered with steel beams and giant pipes, and connected with suspended catwalks.

Barney stopped in front of the complex. The metal casing covering Sunshine clicked and whistled. Barney's body opened up, and she smelled the musty air around her.

"This is the city's power plant. There shouldn't be anything to worry about inside," Barney said as Sunshine climbed out. "The systems running this power plant were automated even before the end days, leaving no reason for even robot workers to tend it."

After taking Bunny from Barney's hand, Sunshine stretched. She was tired of being cramped up inside the robot's body, and despite the smell of the power plant compound, was relieved to be able to move on her own. "Well, where do we go now?"

"Into the core."

"Okey dokey. Let's finish this up, then."

Sunshine followed Barney along the front of the main building. The walls were about three stories tall, without any doors or windows.

"So, how do we get in?" Sunshine asked as she continued walking.

"We go under."

Barney stopped abruptly, and Sunshine bumped into his back. He looked down at a heavy metal disc set in the ground.

"Is that a door?"

"It leads to the sewer."

"Oh, great."

Sunshine watched the metal prongs extend from the robot's hand and into the small holes around the sewer cover. Barney took hold and lifted it without effort. Despite setting it down gently, the cover clanged as it spun on the ground before finally settling.

Sunshine looked down the open hole then squinted up at Barney.

"Is this really the only way inside? I have a feeling that it's gonna be pretty gross down there."

"Don't worry. It hasn't been gross in a very long time."

Sunshine, not waiting for Barney, climbed down into the sewer. Reaching the bottom of the ladder, she peered down a long tunnel lit up by long rows of green lights. The tunnel led straight under the power plant. She was glad that anything ending up down here had dried out long ago.

Barney joined her, his eyes glowing blue and brighter than Momsy's lantern at home. Sunshine spotted something on the ground and rushed to investigate.

"Hey," she said as she picked the thing up. "Look at this weird rock. It looks like a potato."

"That's not a rock," Barney said. "And you should very much put it down."

Sunshine sniffed it, shrugged, and tossed it aside as Barney walked ahead of her. Staying close to the robot, Sunshine looked around the sewer for more weird potato-rocks. Finding none and seeing that she was way behind Barney, she gave up her hunt and ran to join him.

"This tunnel will lead us just outside the core of the power plant," Barney said. "Once we're there, you'll understand what I need you to do."

"Sure. But I don't get how being down here will help me get back home. We're way farther away from the up top than we were at the movie place."

"The power plant has the means to return you to where you belong. Evacuation procedures were put in place in case anything ever went wrong. Once we do what we are here to do, the protocols will respond. Then you'll have your chance to get back home."

"What about you? Are you coming with me?"

Barney stayed quiet for a moment before responding. "This is my world. When it ends, so will I."

"Oh. Um … It'd be okay if you came home with me. Pops likes building things, so I think he'd be pretty okay if a robot came to live with us."

Barney stepped ahead of Sunshine and looked toward the ceiling, his gaze illuminating a large pipe.

"This is it. You'll want to cover your eyes."

Sunshine did and listened to the hum of the robot's laser cutting through the metal. Feeling the heat and an occasional spark hit her, she backed up and waited for him to finish. Once he was done, she peeked and saw he'd made a hole big enough to climb through.

"Right this way," Barney said, holding his arms out to pick her up.

Sunshine let the robot lift her and then climbed the rest of the way into the pipe. After she moved deeper inside, the robot pulled himself up behind her. Sunshine crawled ahead, reaching a right angle where the pipe turned and went straight up into the building.

Now standing, there wasn't enough room for the two of them to go side by side as the vertical pipe went up. There was also nothing to climb to get any higher up.

"Now what?"

"Step here," Barney said.

Sunshine looked down at the robot who was still on all fours in the horizontal part of the pipe. His long ears where moving forward, down toward her feet, and bent in a way that made them look like bicycle pedals. Sunshine stepped onto them.

Feeling herself rise, Sunshine held her hands near the walls of the pipe to keep her balance. She looked up, unable to see what she headed toward. Looking down to Barney, she saw that it was only his ears that were extending.

Sunshine heard engines clanking and rumbling above her as she rose. A little farther up, slivers of light shone into the pipe.

"Almost there," Sunshine whispered down to Barney.

"Good," Barney said. "Just about out of ear."

"What?"

Sunshine felt a jerk and realized she had stopped moving up.

"Oh."

The sliver of light coming through the pipe cover was just out of reach. Sunshine stretched up one hand and could just barely brush it with her finger. Trying to balance on her toes while standing on Barney's ears got her a bit closer, but it still wasn't enough.

"Gotta go a little bit higher!" Sunshine called down.

She looked toward Barney. In the pipe below her, Sunshine couldn't even see his glowing eyes. The ears holding her up shifted. One of her feet slipped from its place, but luckily, the pipe was narrow enough to keep her from falling all the way.

"Sorry!" Barney yelled up. "Need to … "

Sunshine, holding herself up with the help of the pipe walls, started to rise higher. She could feel Barney moving below her, getting up from all fours to give her those last few inches to reach the cover.

Finally, Sunshine was face to face with the thick glass, grimy from whatever once traveled through the pipe. As filthy as it was, the light on the other side was still bright enough to make its way through.

Sunshine examined the cover, looking for a way to open it.

"We could really use your laser saw up here."

"In the middle of something!" Barney yelled, still repositioning himself.

Sunshine pushed the cover, but it didn't budge. Unsure of what to do, she used her sleeve to wipe the glass to at least see what was on the other side.

Most of the smudgy stains cleaned up surprisingly easily, leaving only a light haze on the glass. Sunshine was surprised by the room lit up with bright-white light. It was unlike all the gloominess she had seen outside. It looked clean and undamaged. Everything inside was either white or chrome. Sunshine imagined this is what everything in the dead city might have once looked like.

Then, something moved into her view. Though she assumed, based on everything she had seen so far, that she was seeing another robot, something else about it seemed familiar. The dark figure paced back and forth on four legs, its head down, apparently sniffing.

"Puppy?"

The dog looked up. She pressed her face against the glass, try-ing to see better through the grime. Then, she heard the creature growl.

"Barney," Sunshine whispered. "I don't think we can go in this way."

She felt Barney move beneath her, still in the bottom of the pipe. Catching her balance, she heard the clanging of metal against metal. Barney, doing his best to keep his ears from moving too much, climbed up the pipe.

The dog, now barking, ran toward the pipe's cover. Right on the other side of the glass, it jumped back and forth, fully alert to the trespassers. And then, it started to beep. This was no ordinary dog.

"Barney! We have to go back!"

The robot dog's lower jaw now came completely unhinged in between barking and snapping at the panel that separated it and Sunshine. Its eyes, two tiny red dots, were glaring at Sunshine.

"What's happening?" Barney asked, holding himself in place just below Sunshine.

"They've got a guard dog. Guard-Bot? Dog-Bot?"

"Can it get through? Can we go higher?"

"I don't think so. And no. This is the end."

As she spoke, the dog stopped barking, returning to its growl. As it slowly lowered its head to the glass, Sunshine pushed herself back until she pressed against the other side of the pipe. Then, the dog's nose touched the glass.

Lines of light appeared in the glass, seeming to spread out like veins from where it came in contact with the dog's nose. The nose, made of a simple black mesh just like Barney's, glowed red. Then, the color switched to green.

The glass opened, separating from a seam in the middle that Sunshine hadn't been able to see. The dog's growl was now clear, but it seemed to wane as the dog sniffed the scent coming from the pipe. As the panel opened all the way, Sunshine came face to face with the snarling robot dog.

The dog backed away and stared at Sunshine. Despite its rigid metal face, it looked confused. Sunshine knew that it must have been an eternity since the dog had seen any human in the factory, and she tried to keep still, hoping that it wouldn't think of her as a threat.

"Hi, puppy," Sunshine said in her most gentle voice. Reaching into her pouch, she grabbed a handful of burned popcorn and held it out to the dog. "You want a little snack?"

The dog approached slowly and sniffed Sunshine's hand. Then, tucking its head down, it backed away.

Sunshine shrugged. "All right, then. Well, could you help me get out of here?"

The robot dog bent down to its front paws and reached its head into the pipe. Sunshine grabbed onto its muzzle. As it pulled her out, she heard Barney clanging along behind her.

"Thanks," Sunshine said, sitting on the floor. "I'm Sunshine. This is Bunny. And that's Barney. They're both rabbits, but Barney's a robot, so it's pretty different."

The dog looked to Sunshine then Barney. As they stared at each other, there was a long silence. Then, at the same time, both robots began clicking, beeping, and whistling at each other.

Barney turned to Sunshine.

"This is Rusty. He's here to make sure no one touches anything. This may be a problem."

"Oh. Well. You can't get him to help?"

"Not yet. But he'll give us a tour. It should lead us to the core."

"Okay. Maybe you can do your robo-talk some more and let him know what's going on."

"Already did. Unfortunately, since he's always been here, he's unaware of just how bad things are."

"Hmm," Sunshine said in an exaggerated tone, scratching her chin.

Sunshine walked up to the dog and patted it on the head.

"Rusty, I need you to take us to the core. We have to do some stuff that I'm not super sure of so that I can get back home. Barney says it'll turn off the all the power in the city, but that'll help keep anyone else from ending up stuck down here. That'd help make sure nobody comes around to touch any of your fancy machines. Can you help us out?"

Rusty barked, his voice raspy and not sounding anything like an actual dog.

"Good," Sunshine said to Rusty. Then, turning to Barney, "See? No problemo."

Sunshine and Barney followed Rusty out of the first room. The white corridor glowed in bright contrast to the world outside the power plant. Sunshine ran her hand against the wall, expecting at least a little bit of grime, but there was none. Instead, lights beneath the wall appeared where she touched, as though the electricity inside was just waiting for somewhere to go after ages of sitting idle within the dead city.

The corridor ended, branching off in two directions of a curved passageway, which appeared to wrap around a large central room.

"This is it," Barney said. "On the other side of this wall is the core. We should be able to find an entrance if we go in either—"

Something crashed far behind them and continued to crash as it tore through the building. Like a deafening siren, Rusty howled. Sunshine looked down the corridor they had just come from, seeing nothing but hearing every sort of destruction headed their way.

"He's found us," Sunshine said, knowing what was coming.

Rounding the corner, the Usher-Bot's arms flailed, smashing against everything around it and sending bolts of electricity flying. Its digital face scowled at Sunshine. The Concessionaughts followed it.

"Run!" Barney yelled.

While Rusty charged the monsters from the cinema, Sunshine ran around the dome. She could hear the familiar sound of Barney's laser followed by the chorus of "Let's all go to the lobby" broken by shrill screams.

The passageway curved and came to another, larger hall. A doorway led inside the dome. It was closed, and she feared it was also locked.

The sound of the robot battle was now far behind her, and she could hear only the occasional explosion as she searched the door for a way in. On one side she found a panel with a single button containing four hollowed-out parts. It resembled a dog paw.

Sunshine looked back down the hall. The few crashes she was still able to hear grew fewer and farther between, just like the popcorn had when every kernel was just about popped. Knowing what she had to do, Sunshine started running back the way she'd come.

Barney pulled Rusty out of a cloud of black smoke. The silver hare turned his attention to Sunshine, his eyes flashing red and amber.

"Run!" Barney screamed.

From the cloud of smoke, Sunshine heard clanging and banging coming closer. One metal tentacle, then another, whipped into view.

"The show must go on," a familiar voice rasped.

# Lost Tomorrow

# Feature Presentation

Metal tentacles pulled the Usher-Bot out from the smoke and dust, and Sunshine looked on in terror at what it had become. Steel bands twisted around it. Parts of the Concessionaughts were welded to the Usher-Bot's torso. The outer shell of the giant soda cup was ripped into long sharp strands that spiraled around the Usher-Bot like some sort of jagged armor. Half of the face of the popcorn box sat on top of the Usher-Bot's head like a crown.

"This way, you guys!" Sunshine yelled.

Getting Rusty to his feet, Barney pulled the robot dog down the hall toward Sunshine. The Usher-Bot howled, its tentacles flailing, smashing against the walls of the dome. As Barney reached Sunshine, he picked her up, setting her on top of Rusty.

Rusty burst into top speed, but before he rounded the bend in the hall, Sunshine looked back. The Usher-Bot stood still, smoke and sparks spitting out from its upgraded body. It stared at her, not chasing, just waiting.

Sunshine felt the wind rush by her as Rusty ran. Reaching the door of the dome, she slid off the robot dog. She spotted the door's keypad.

"This one's on you, Rusty," she said.

When Rusty placed his paw on the pad, the door retracted into a hidden recess. Sunshine ran inside but then froze, her toes just beyond the entrance.

The dome was massive. Metal girders wrapped all around the top to hold the structure together, but the floor was absent. The walls rose high above her to the top of the dome, but they went even farther downward, like a silo sprouting up from a bottomless pit.

A steel bridge stretched from the doorway where Sunshine stood toward a platform in the center. On it stood a giant cylinder of bright-orange liquid with red splotches within it. Computers and monitors tracking all the hundreds of readings given off by a power plant of this magnitude surrounded the cylinder.

Looking back, Rusty stood in the doorway.

"What are you doing?" Sunshine shouted.

Rusty turned away from Sunshine and looked down the hall. Then, looking at Barney, the dog clicked and clacked in the chatter of their robot language.

"I understand," Barney said.

"What? Why isn't he coming?"

"It's his core programming. His purpose is to prevent humans from touching anything. He would be forced to stop what we need to do here."

"But the movie monster! He's gonna get smashed up if he stays out there."

Barney looked at Rusty and then continued across the bridge.

"It will be okay. He understands what must be done."

Sunshine watched the door close, shutting Rusty out on the other side. While the crashing sound of the Usher-Bot came closer, she turned toward the platform in the center of the dome.

"It doesn't matter," Barney said. "Once we finish what we're here to do, all the remaining robots will finally power down forever."

Sunshine ran to the platform, jumping over the step leading from the bridge. The machines around her hummed and chirped, their sounds calm compared to the chaos she had just escaped. Inside the orange liquid in the cylinder, red splotches slowly drifted up and down, like oil in water that refused to mix.

At the base of the cylinder, a control panel wrapped all the way around it. Like the entrance to the dome, there was a panel made for a handprint. But unlike the one outside, this was made for a human.

"This is why you needed me," Sunshine said, turning to Barney. "You need a person to shut everything down."

Barney nodded, and his paw pointed at a capsule standing on edge of the platform. The capsule looked like a giant blue pea pod with glass windows. It was large enough for a grown-up to step inside.

"In case of emergency," Barney said, opening a cabinet beside one of the consoles, "that would be a human's means of escape. Once activated, the capsule drains the power it needs to operate then continues to sap the remaining power from the city in order to prevent catastrophic meltdown. The capsule is a teleporter. It will move the operator to a safe distance during whatever incident may arise. In this case, it should send you back home, out of range of the city."

"Should?"

"Don't worry. I can set a precise location." He pulled a box from the cabinet and handed it to Sunshine. "Put these on."

Sunshine opened the box and pulled out a strange pair of glasses with one red and one blue lens. Putting them on, she looked at the teleporter. At first, everything in her vision seemed to pop out like it was only inches away, but then it returned to normal and even the different-colored lenses seemed to merge to one hue.

"Are you sure you want me to do this? I know that you're robots and you're not really alive, but you still kind of are."

Barney nodded. "Sunshine. We have been here for hundreds of years, sitting still; not waiting for the city to become what it once was, just sitting. This place isn't ours to rebuild. We were only ever meant to serve the human residents. They're all gone now. As you've seen, time has corrupted some of us, leaving us desperate to serve those who happen to fall into this place. This is a danger that could last forever if something isn't done to stop it."

Sunshine shook her head at the thought of destroying this world, even if most of the work was already done for her.

"But," Sunshine said, "you're my friend."

"It's okay. I am only a robot."

Sunshine disagreed, but her hand hovered above the panel, ready to initiate the end of the underground world. Squeezing Bunny under the other arm, Sunshine knew what she had to do. She held her breath as her hand slammed down, pressing the handprint panel.

The chirps and clicking of the machines around her stopped, replaced by a hum. Sunshine, keeping her hand on the panel, saw letters and numbers appear from nowhere, floating all around her in the air.

Sunshine lifted her hand and stepped away from the panel. Pushing the hovering letters and numbers aside, she walked through the language of the machine. She didn't understand what she was looking for, but somehow she knew some piece of code existed, waiting for her to find it.

"The teleporter," Barney said. "You need to redirect the power of the city to the teleporter."

Sunshine turned and looked at the capsule. Light swirled around it, holding geometric shapes and equations that she had never seen in the math work that Pops had taught her. The glowing digits didn't seem to make any sense as they spun around each other, but then, as Sunshine walked into the digital cloud, she started to understand.

Sunshine held her hand up. Like some kind of inexplicable magic, the code moved, following her will. With her other hand, she lifted Bunny up to the digital chaos, and more of it flowed the way she wanted.

Spinning around, Sunshine used her mind to reorganize giant swaths of the code through the air. The interior of the dome brightened, and Sunshine squinted, trying to see what exactly she had done to hack the system. Just beyond the letters and numbers in the air, she saw that it wasn't her that had filled the room with light.

Lost in the trance of the machine language, she hadn't heard them coming. Sunshine caught a glimpse of the dome's door flying above the railing of the bridge and into the pit below. The Usher-Bot, fused with the freaky Concessionaughts, slowly twitched its way toward the platform. Then, she spied something that nearly broke her connection with the code.

At one end of the Usher-Bot's tentacle, Rusty was held by the top of the head. Helpless, the robot dog struggled in the monster's grasp. White light burst from the dog's eyes.

Letters, numbers, and symbols she had yet to learn coursed through Rusty's eyes. The Usher-Bot was corrupting Rusty's programming, just like she was doing to the power plant and teleporter. She watched the code, reading the changes that were being made, understanding what was happening. It was too late for Rusty, and if she didn't hurry, it would be too late for her. Fortunately, Sunshine now knew what she was capable of.

The Usher-Bot released Rusty, letting him fall onto the bridge. The white light in his eyes faded to black.

"It's time for our feature presentation," the Usher-Bot growled.

"Rusty," Sunshine said in a whisper. She watched the robot dog twitch and twist its head toward her, rising beside its new master.

"You have to hurry," Barney said, snapping Sunshine's attention out of the overwhelming sight of the dog. "This is why we——"

Sunshine heard something snap just as Barney's voice was cut off. Terror rushed through her as metal tentacles wrapped around the silver hare.

"Barney!" Sunshine yelled. "Run!"

Barney tried to flee, his body buzzing, shaking, and twisting to release himself. As he darted in one direction, he whipped back to where he started. There was no escaping the grasp of the Usher-Bot.

Barney charged up for another attempt, a final burst of all his power. Sunshine, ignoring the zeroes and ones in the air, watched, waiting, hoping to see Barney run faster than anything had ever run and snap the tentacles right off the robot that wanted to imprison them both. Barney's eyes glowed bright white. Sunshine knew he was ready. Then, before he could make his escape, the tentacles released him.

"Return back home?" the Usher-Bot asked, his voice surprisingly calm.

Sunshine looked past Barney. The Usher-Bot stood still, lights around its face monitor pulsing slowly.

"I saw. Inside this one's memory. You are trying to return home," the Usher-Bot said, now staring at Sunshine. "To return to your family."

Sunshine nodded.

"This machine. This teleporter … It can transport the people below to the people above … "

Sunshine shrugged then nodded once again.

"To return you to your parents … humans … There are … more humans still alive."

Sunshine stepped back.

"It could bring the world below to the world above."

Sunshine backed up against the control panel of the teleporter.

"It could bring the world above to the world below. It could bring the rest of living humanity to us. To the movies. To a sellout show!

To the movies! Sellout show! Sellout show!"

Sunshine spun around, her hand flying through the code. She heard the Usher-Bot step onto the platform and knew she had to hurry. Rusty barked and glared at her with black eyes, corrupted by the Usher-Bot's reprogramming. She pressed button after button on the panel with one hand, still using the other to hack the system. Sunshine tried to read the code, tried to understand what she was doing, and how to get the machine to work before the Usher-Bot could get ahold of it for its own use.

Sunshine's world froze as the tentacle slammed into the control panel. She turned to see the Usher-Bot on the other side of the platform. Everything—the robots, the flashing lights, the zeroes and ones floating around her—moved in slow motion. Barney was on the panel. The clockwork hare rose to his feet, eyes still glowing white.

Barney ran, a silver streak trailing behind him. Standing between her and the Usher-Bot, Barney looked up to Sunshine. He pointed to a cluster of code floating high to Sunshine's right. As she looked at it, the digits glowed brighter than those around them. Barney pointed to another group, this one hovering beside the Usher-Bot. Sunshine reached out her hand and pulled the clusters together.

As Barney pointed out a third group, she finally recognized the pattern. She couldn't hear herself, she couldn't feel herself doing it, but Sunshine laughed like a maniac.

Sunshine's hands waved through the air, making the code swirl around them. Clusters of zeroes and ones merged together, and the platform's machines rumbled to life. As she worked, the Usher-Bot remained still, frozen in place. Though she felt like she moved slowly, Sunshine knew she was moving like Barney, probably leaving nothing but a purple streak in her wake along with the blue blur of Bunny as she swung him through the code.

Just beyond the code, the tiniest splash of dark liquid burst upward in slow motion. Above it, Rusty snapped his jaws, sending motor oil flying. Though he was still far from her, and moving slower than she was, the corrupted machine gained ground, letting the digits in the air roll off him as he made progress toward his target.

Sunshine watched the dog rush forward, and a cool calm washed over her. With the wave of a hand, she sent a stream of code into Rusty. With time moving as slowly as it was, there was no way for her to see if her hack had stopped him.

Both Sunshine and Barney flung their hands straight up. The code spiraled around them and funneled to the capsule in the center of the platform. As the teleporter powered up, Sunshine felt electricity surging in from the world around her, pouring into the machine that would take her home.

"Go," Barney said, turning to the Usher-Bot.

As the silver hare turned, everything that had seemed motionless now whirred back to life. Air rushed into Sunshine's lungs, and she knew that, whatever she had just done, it had worked. Then, she saw Rusty curled up on the floor of the platform. The dog looked up casually at her and then tucked his head back between his paws. Sunshine smiled. She had undone the Usher-Bot's corruption.

Behind her, something snapped. Looking back just in time, Sunshine ducked, dodging the control panel as it was ripped up by the tentacles of the Usher-Bot.

"Restless children will be silenced!"

"Go!" Barney yelled.

Sunshine ran to the capsule and jumped inside, burying Bunny's head against her as the world around them tore itself apart. The Usher-Bot's tentacles ripped the bridge from its place, leaving the capsule as the only means of escape. Sunshine watched the robot lurch toward her. Trapped inside with nowhere to run, she looked around for something, anything, to activate the machine and send her home. Then, she felt the capsule shake as two of the Usher-Bot's tentacles clasped it.

Barney erupted into a silver streak, crashing into the Usher-Bot and sending both of them flying. Oil burst from the tentacles as they tore free. Sunshine raised her arm to avoid the splatter, but looking up, she felt her heart sink.

The remaining arms of the Usher-Bot had Barney in their grasp. While she watched in terror, the interior of the capsule started to glow.

Sunshine felt the capsule working. She became lighter. Everything inside her seemed to be coming apart, just like Barney at the hands of the Usher-Bot. But then, she realized she wasn't a helpless onlooker.

Sunshine raised her hand in front of her to find that it had already started to dematerialize. It didn't matter. She still had control. The code, still floating in the air, was hers.

With a wave of her hand, Sunshine reached into the code. It surrounded the Usher-Bot and Barney. Wrapping the code around the tentacles of the crazed robot, she ripped its arms off of Barney, letting the silver hare fall free to the ground. Barney turned back.

"It doesn't matter!" he yelled. "You have to get out of here! Drain the rest of the power, and go!"

"Not yet," Sunshine said, her voice calm amid the chaos.

The Usher-Bot screamed something incoherent and filled with static. Its tentacles lashed the ground, and it sprang forward, charging at Sunshine.

Sunshine closed her fist; the zeroes and ones tightened around the Usher-Bot and locked it in place. She could feel the electricity inside it draining out, transferring to the teleporter. Not only was her way home now fully charged, the Usher-Bot was finished.

As the menace from the movies fell to the platform, the Usher-Bot stared at her, the face on its monitor twitching in and out of static.

"Enjoy your show," it said, its voice slow and followed by a series of beeps until nothing was left.

"It's time," Barney said as Rusty slumped alongside him.

Sunshine nodded. Raising her hand, which was nearly transparent, she moved the floating digits to whirl around the last remaining robots. It wrapped around them. She could feel their programming become one with the cloud of code. As their energy transferred into the teleporter, the zeroes and ones filled her vision, making the world glow a bright yellow green. Then, everything went black.

Sunshine blinked her eyes open and saw traces of code floating over her. She swatted at the air, trying to dismiss the remaining illusions. As she did, she realized everything around her had changed.

With Bunny in one hand, she used the other to push herself up. Between her fingers, she felt the soft squish of mud and the crunch of twigs. A beam of sunlight shone brightly in her face, but she was in a tight, dark space. She looked around at the dirty ground, wooden walls, and claw marks. She knew right where she was.

"Sunshine!" a voice called out.

Sunshine crawled out of the hollow tree and rubbed her eyes, trying to adjust them to the afternoon sun in Ballihag Bog.

"There you are," Momsy said. "You look like you've been dealing with bog monsters this whole time."

"Cut it out," Sunshine said, running up to Momsy and jumping into her arms. "Did you miss me? Did you guys have to camp out here while I was gone? Did you have to go to town to gather up a search party? Did you run into the bog monster? I didn't find any. What about robots? Did you see any robots?"

"What? No, of course not. You did miss lunch, though. How long do you think you were napping?"

"Napping?"

"Hey, sleepyhead," Pops said, appearing from the other side of the bog monster's tree.

"I wasn't taking a nap," Sunshine said as she climbed down from Momsy's arms. "I was saving the world from robots that want to force us to watch movies and feed us burned popcorn."

"You're a strange kid," Pops said, wiping the mud off Sunshine's back. "Let's head home. We saved you some beans to munch on the way."

Sunshine shrugged and skipped along behind Pops and Momsy. As she followed them down the path, she glanced back at the tree, the entrance to another world. She had come here expecting a bog monster, but had found a long-dead city instead. Despite what her foster parents thought, she knew it was real. After all, she could still feel the ash and grime on the movie ticket in her pocket.

The End ...
... for now

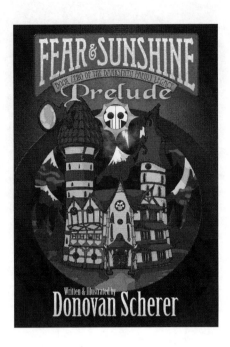

*Are you ready to enter a world of monsters and mad science?*

## Fear & Sunshine: Prelude is yours for free.

For generations, the Darksmith family has constructed, concocted, or otherwise created the most menacing monstrosities the world has ever known. While the art of mad science is their business, the danger of serving the forces of darkness is always present, waiting to strike.

However, this is only the beginning as a new generation is about to be welcomed into the world of things that go bump in the night.

*Visit www.DonovanScherer.com/Prelude*
*to get the free ebook*

# Other Books by Donovan Scherer

You can find an up to date list of all my books at:

www.DonovanScherer.com/MyBooks

### The Fear & Sunshine Series
### A Saga of Monsters, Mad Science, and a Little Hippie Girl

Book Zero - Fear & Sunshine: Prelude

Book One - Fear & Sunshine

Book Two - Fear & Sunshine: Dark Matters

### Other Stories I've Written

Monsters Around the Campfire

### Other Stories I've Illustrated

Hello, Halloween by Luke J. Morris

Tales from the Terrible Scary by Guy Incognito

*Want to know a secret?*

If you enjoy this book and have developed
an insatiable taste for more monsters, you can
get a FREE ebook copy of another one of my books
by leaving a review. I won't tell you which one, though.
It's a secret. To find out, click or visit:

*www.DonovanScherer.com/Secret*

# About the Author

I'm Donovan Scherer, an author and illustrator creating worlds of adventure with a sense of humor and a little bit of dread that everything will go terribly, terribly wrong. I tend to think in cartoon, but since animation would take me longer than I'd like to keep you waiting on my stories, I write and illustrate them instead.

You can find all the places I'm at online at:
www.DonovanScherer.com/Online

Made in the USA
San Bernardino, CA
22 February 2016